All's *Fair* in *Love* & *Seduction*

BEVERLEY KENDALL

ALL'S FAIR IN LOVE & SEDUCTION
Beverley Kendall
Copyright © Beverley Kendall 2015
Published by Season Publishing LLC

This is a work of fiction. Names, characters, places and incidents are products of the author's imagination or are used fictitiously and are not to be construed as real. Any resemblance to actual events, locales, organizations, or persons, living or dead, is completely coincidental.

www.beverleykendall.com
Cover Design © The Killion Group, Inc.

DEDICATION

To Ryan, I love you (this much) to infinity and beyond.

ACKNOWLEDGMENTS

To the greatest CPs a girl can have. Anastasia, your insight and knack for detail are invaluable. Barb, to the best blurb and query reviser ever. Thank you.

ALSO BY BEVERLEY KENDALL

HISTORICAL ROMANCE
The Elusive Lords Series

SINFUL SURRENDER
A TASTE OF DESIRE
AN HEIR OF DECEPTION

CONNECTING SERIES
The Temptresses

TWICE THE TEMPTATION

NEW ADULT ROMANCE
Unforgettable You

ONLY FOR YOU
ALL OVER YOU (short novel)
ALWAYS BEEN YOU

CONNECTING SERIES
Trapped

THE TRAP (FREE DIGITAL PREQUEL)
TRAPPED
TRAPPED EXPANDED EDITION (INCLUDES THE TRAP)

CHAPTER ONE

"Who is that standing next to Lady Windmere?" Lord Derek Creswell asked while his gaze remained fixed on the dark-haired beauty casting furtive glances at him over a lovely bare shoulder.

Derek had first glimpsed her at the Radcliffe ball the month past. Since then, he'd seen her at various other society events.

And he wouldn't mind seeing much more of her.

Lord Alex Cartwright angled his head in the direction of Derek's stare and replied curtly, "Miss Elizabeth Smith."

Normally, Derek would have wasted no time in seeking an introduction but something had cautioned against it. Perhaps it was the incongruity of innocence and sensuality packaged in a female form meant to make a man think of sin and nothing else.

By God, he'd been tempted, no doubt about that, but since he'd stopped letting his cock take the lead in all things soft and female, he'd had to be content to admire her from afar.

"And?" Derek prompted, his attention still focused wholly on Miss Smith. It appeared the task of eliciting information from his friend would be an arduous one.

After a pause, Cartwright relented, replying as if reading points on a list. "Miss Elizabeth Smith. She's Missy's cousin twice removed. Her father recently came into a barony. This is her first Season."

Lady Windmere's cousin and thereby Rutherford's relation—though somewhat distant—by marriage.

Of all the bloody luck.

This made the situation particularly sticky if he chose to pursue her. He had to decide whether she was worth the headache of incurring Rutherford's wrath should things not go to the lady's satisfaction.

"She *is* stunning," Derek remarked offhandedly in a belated and weak attempt to play down his interest.

Light brown eyes, red bow-shaped lips and skin like silk; almost as if she had been fashioned specifically with men in mind.

Derek had wanted her from the first time he'd seen her and tonight that want had become a relentless throb in his loins. He knew what that meant and like the departure of a long treasured friend, he bade a silent farewell to his good judgment.

"That she is," Cartwright replied, his voice softening and somewhat bemused.

Perturbed, Derek shot him a quick glance, then turned and followed the direction of his friend's narrowed gaze to discover Cartwright wasn't looking at Miss Smith at all. His friend's attention centered on one of the Rutherford twins. From that distance, Derek couldn't tell which as they appeared to be identical in every way save temperament. He imagined it was Charlotte, the quieter one, for there had always been an undercurrent of something between them. He hadn't exactly known what but it was obvious now.

Lust. Passion. Affection?

For his friend's sake Derek hoped he felt a healthy dose of the latter, she was Rutherford's cousin by blood after all, raised by him since the age of fifteen. There existed a bond between them Rutherford wouldn't have with his wife's cousin. Not that Rutherford would stand to see Miss Smith trifled with.

Regardless, Derek was relieved his friend's interest was not in Miss Smith. It wouldn't do for them to be lusting after the same woman.

Derek returned his attention to Miss Smith and as if he'd willed it by the force of his gaze, she angled her head to peep at him for the fifth time since he'd arrived a half hour ago. Her eyes widened at his openly admiring regard, for in the past he'd been just as circumspect as she in their visual intercourse.

Their eyes met and held, and the awareness that had smoldered like a brush fire between them, threatened to burst into a conflagration of lust. Seconds ticked too slowly, too quickly before she looked away, her face flushed a violent pink. A heaviness settled in his loins.

"Arrange an introduction," Derek demanded quietly, giving up all presence of casual interest.

Cartwright slanted a glance in his direction, one eyebrow rising above a lock of black hair resting low on his forehead. He did not immediately respond, instead appeared to be thoughtfully choosing his words. "I've met her…Miss Smith. She is not the worldly sort. And more to the point, she is practically Rutherford's relation. If you're looking for a dalliance, I think it best you set your sights elsewhere."

How had Cartwright taken it as far as dalliance when he'd merely asked for an introduction? It wasn't as if he meant to whisk her off to the gardens for a private ravishing. At least not that very night.

Caught!

The sheer weight of Lord Creswell's regard initially made it impossible for Elizabeth to look away. His gaze pierced her through to her core, creating an ache that started in her chest and spiraled downward until her inner thighs clenched in an effort to contain it, find relief from it, only to find none.

After several breathless moments trapped under the heat of his penetrating stare, she summoned up what little of her will remained, managing to wrench her gaze away.

An image of him as he'd looked six years ago pushed to the forefront of her thoughts. He had been the kind of handsome that warranted second and third looks. But that first impression he'd made upon her fifteen-year-old heart paled in comparison to what he did to it now.

He'd grown only more handsome in the ensuing years, his dark hair cut shorter, his shoulders broader, his cheekbones more pronounced and jaw more squared. He

4

had an air of maturity in his face that had been lacking in the twenty-three year-old man who had stood in her parents' parlor, venom in his eyes and condemnation lacing his every word. Before her now—not but thirty feet away—was a man who would stand out in any crowd. In the prime of his youth, he wore his black and white tailored garments with the same ease as he carried himself. Before her stood a man of consequence; a man she could only gaze upon but never even think to have for her own.

The viscount didn't know who she was and provided she kept her distance, he never would. But given the small and exclusive nature of the London ton, their paths would undoubtedly cross again. The prospect should have given her pause instead of causing an unwanted thrill to shoot through her.

"He is quite handsome is he not?"

Charlotte's voice jolted Elizabeth from her thoughts that ever increasingly tended to center on the viscount.

"Who?" Elizabeth tried her hand at nonchalance but feared the effect was lost to the heat flooding her face. Her mother often said she wore her heart on her sleeve and one day it would be her undoing. If she should come undone, best it occur after her first London Season, well out of the vicinity of prying eyes and loose tongues.

"Alex," Charlotte chided, with the ease of a friendship that numbered in years and not the month since their introduction.

It had taken the better part of only three days after

Elizabeth arrived at Laurel House before Charlotte had confided her feelings for Lord Alex—infatuation-turned-to-love that now spanned three years.

After meeting Lord Alex, Elizabeth wasn't the least bit surprised. With his piercing silver-gray eyes and dimple in his chin, the second son of the Duke of Hastings possessed looks and charm to spare. Truth be told, he and Lord Creswell shared a superficial resemblance, both tall and handsome, each with a thick black head of hair.

"Very handsome indeed," Elizabeth agreed with a sage nod. She flitted another glance in the men's direction but the group at their side had shifted. The back of Lord Stanton's silver-streaked head now obstructed her view and his voice boomed, threatening to render her deaf in one ear.

"He is a good friend of Alex's. I can arrange an introduction if you'd like."

The offer was tempting. Elizabeth had dreamt of their meeting since her mother had informed her she was to have a London Season. Her father's title had not only come with two entailed properties but a stipend of three thousand a year. A veritable fortune to a family who had thus existed in something close to genteel poverty.

"I'm certain Lord Creswell is deluged with admirers," she replied evasively. Any sane woman would leap at the chance to meet the rich, handsome viscount, and the state of her mental acuity had up until that day, never been questioned. She'd very much like it to remain that way.

Charlotte chortled, the sound light and ebullient, which

had Elizabeth chuckling in spite of herself. "You are quite right. He's a particular favorite of the ladies."

Their laughter faded under a companionable silence before Elizabeth spoke again. "Where can Catherine have got to?" She hoped her friend didn't note and file the change of subject for precisely what it was.

Her question had the desired effect for Charlotte immediately went up on her toes and began scouring the room for her twin. A mass of golden curls secured loosely at her crown with pale pink hair combs bobbed as she twisted her neck from right to left and back again.

Situated at the rear of the estate, the ballroom stretched the entire width of the main house with the dance floor taking up a third of that acreage. A refreshment room conveniently adjoined the dance floor and four sets of French doors opened out onto a stone terrace. The private garden beyond was said to be one of the most beautiful in all of London.

The last they had seen Catherine, Sir William Kingsley had come to claim her for a dance. The set had finished some five minutes ago but as London was experiencing a July devoid of the rain that sometimes plagued the summer month, perhaps he had taken her outside for a stroll.

"She must have—" Charlotte began but broke off when she saw Lord Alex approaching. Apparently, women were rendered speechless in the presence of gentleman with excessive good looks—particularly the ones they happened to be in love with.

7

"Charlotte." From his lips, her name was a greeting, a familiar address...and something more. His head dipped in a bow but his eyes never left her.

Charlotte stood momentarily mute, transfixed as her blue eyes drank him in. And not in huge gulps but in savoring sips, as if she'd learned not to gorge herself. Elizabeth could have been a piece of furniture for all the attention the two paid her.

Then as if remembering Elizabeth's no doubt unfortunate presence and his own usually impeccable manners, Lord Alex shifted his focus smoothly to her. "Good evening, Miss Smith. I hope you're enjoying yourself."

"Thank you, my lord. I'm having a fine time." How fortunate Charlotte was to have captured the affections of such a man for it was obvious her friend's feelings were duly returned.

"Alex." Charlotte's belated greeting sounded like a breathless sigh, her pleasure as transparent as the polished crystal glasses used to serve the wine and champagne.

For several seconds, very little could be heard above the haunting notes of the waltz and the collective rumble of three hundred guests. The small circle they had formed in the back of the room fell into the kind of silence that brought about a lot of throat clearing and fidgeting of fingers and toes. Inclined to the latter on such occasions, Elizabeth found herself smoothing the lace edge on her blue satin skirts.

"My friend has abandoned me for the greater

outdoors." Lord Alex broke the thick silence, motioning with his head toward the gray London night beyond the terrace doors. "And suddenly I found myself surrounded by dewy-faced debutantes."

Elizabeth noted the imperceptible stiffening of Charlotte's form. Pleasure faded from her eyes. "So you are using us to escape." Her tone made it an indictment, her pursed lips a rebuke.

Lord Alex's smile faltered and his brow furrowed, clearly taken aback by her charge. Before he could open his mouth to ask the nature of his transgression, Elizabeth excused herself, pleading heat, thirst and hunger, any of which would be true. She hurried away with no true destination in mind just the knowledge that she was superfluous to any situation with Charlotte and Lord Alex in each other's company.

Mr. Peter Finley was the next name on her dance card but before she returned to the floor for the next set she could use a breath of fresh air. Well it wouldn't be terribly fresh. This was London after all. But it would have to do until she returned to the much cleaner Wilton air.

My friend has abandoned me for the greater outdoors.

The statement taunted her...lured her as she escaped the ballroom and stepped out onto the lit terrace. What she was doing was foolhardy, her actions putting her vaunted mental acuity under question.

But, she reasoned, she was one of the many Smiths in a city teeming with Smiths, Smyths and Smythes. With her widowed sister living in Dorchester and her parents in

Wilton overseeing the renovations of their new residence, what reason would the viscount have to connect her with them?

None.

So what possible harm could come from a chance encounter at a party hosted by the estimable Lord and Lady Windmere?

No harm at all.

A rash of gooseflesh appeared when the cool night air struck the skin of her upper arms. Elizabeth gave an involuntary shiver as she took in the long stretch of the terrace, which sat as desolate and silent as the Yorkshire moors. She had expected to see Lord Creswell there in a wide-legged stance, a cheroot in his mouth and a trail of gray smoke rising up to mingle with the equally gray London air that settled above the city like a dark shroud.

Behind a six-tiered stone fountain where water trickled from the mouth of a playful dolphin, the garden landscaped into a maze of lofty hedgerows, shrubs of honeysuckle, and neat rows of yellow daisies and red roses. Toward the back of the property, three large elms offered shade to a white gazebo.

The scent of honeysuckle competed with the dank air and tonight was winning handily. Elizabeth inhaled the sweet fragrance deeply into her lungs as she ventured to the edge of the garden.

Slowly, she looked around and rolled up onto her toes in hopes of spying the viscount's dark head above the first hedgerow. But for the buzz and chirps of nocturnal insects and the leaves rustling in the breeze, Elizabeth concluded she was quite alone.

"Where did he go?" she muttered to herself. Disappointed, she came down hard on the heels of her satin evening shoes.

"Were you looking for someone in particular?" drawled a deep masculine voice from behind her.

CHAPTER TWO

Elizabeth spun around so quickly she lost her footing and stumbled headlong—well actually breast-first if she was striving for accuracy—into the hard wall of a male chest. Large hands shot out to steady her, his hold firm yet gentle on her arms. Elizabeth snatched her hands away from his chest and took a hasty step back.

Surely, fate would not be so cruel…? She peered up and encountered the arresting blue-green eyes of Lord Creswell.

Fate had a most unfortunate sense of humor.

"My lord, you frightened me." Surprise may have caused her to stumble but it was the man who left her breathless.

And it wasn't just his masculine beauty; she'd like to think she wasn't that shallow. No, it was more than that. He had an aura of confidence about him—some might say arrogance—that drew women with the same pull the sun exerted on the Earth.

"I'm sorry. Please accept my apologies," he said, all politesse and unimpeachable decorum. But his hooded gaze and the way his mouth twitched at the corners told her he wasn't the slightest bit sorry at all.

Elizabeth had no doubt the viscount knew it was he she'd been searching for. He'd heard her. Heat flooded her face. She could only imagine what he thought of her.

Her mother had also warned that her impetuous nature would one day land her in a heap of trouble. Trouble of this sort must follow the viscount about like a starving mongrel in search of table scraps.

Truly, if she had a mite bit of sense where he was concerned, she would return inside now that her curiosity had been quenched. She'd seen him, spoken to him, touched him even; that should be enough. And if she were lucky, he'd never discover she was a member of the same Smith family his father had paid one thousand pounds to quiet her parents' cries for his brother to redress her sister's honor.

"I-I didn't expect to find anyone out here." Elizabeth nearly groaned in dismay at such an obvious lie. At affairs such as this, gardens weren't merely a floral feast for the eyes but also provided a haven for lovers seeking privacy from the crush, and tall and dense foliage proved the perfect shield to share a kiss and other such intimacies.

Lord Creswell continued to study her with slumberous eyes. Silence dragged along at a tortuous pace and with every second that ticked by, Elizabeth's discomfort climbed. She wished he would say *something*.

Finally, he smiled a slow devilish grin, his gaze drifting from her face to her neckline before dipping lower. He paused there, lingering long enough to offend— if a woman would be offended by the lustful stare of a

13

handsome man. Slowly, he lifted his regard back to hers. "And I hoped you were looking for me."

A wave of arousal, the likes of which Elizabeth had never known, washed over her. She went from warm to burning hot in the span of seconds.

"I came out for some air." Her voice was breathy and uneven.

Liar. The silent rejoinder was brutally swift and damning.

The word remained unspoken but was there in his too knowing eyes and the soft laugh that rumbled from his throat.

"How utterly remarkable as I too came out for...*air*. I think it would be prudent if we took air together. Would that please you, Miss Smith?" He advanced a step. He now stood close enough for her to make out dark stubble beginning to shadow his jaw. His shoulders blocked the gaslight illuminating the terrace.

Did he truly believe she would *take air* with a man she'd only just met?

But of course he did, and she could hardly blame him given her actions. There were names for women like that.

Elizabeth Ann Smith?

No, despite what he thought or how it might appear, she was not that type of woman even if the temptation to throw off the rigid strictures of society acted upon her like a virulent disease.

Elizabeth affected an airy sophisticated laugh, attempting to hide what she prayed wasn't too obvious;

that she was unaccustomed to the kind of flirtatious banter he no doubt excelled at. "My lord, we *are* taking air together."

"No, not yet but I'm sure we will soon." This time his tone did not tease. His expression sobered as he eyed her mouth with more than avid interest.

Elizabeth felt as if a fire had been ignited inside her. However, the other part of her, the daughter of Richard Smith with his rigid moral code and God-fearing ways felt compelled to say something. Indeed, something that would convey a bit of umbrage at his cheek. A young lady in her position would not be aroused by such provocation. In fact, she would be quite outraged. They were strangers after all.

"My lord," she began, "I really must take—"

"Derek. Lord Derek Creswell. But then I'm certain you know precisely who I am. And I would like to know you, Miss Elizabeth Smith." The velvet smoothness of his voice strummed her senses like the premier virtuoso of seduction.

Elizabeth's mouth snapped closed.

He knew her name. More importantly, he had inquired about her.

Swallowing was made all the more difficult with the complete obstruction of her throat. Her heart began to beat double time.

He watched her as if he liked nothing better than to have his wicked way with her. Her nipples peaked and the place between her thighs grew moist in her own wicked response. But no matter how tempting the offer in his eyes, she could not encourage him. A union between them was impossible.

A small step backward began her retreat as her mind strived for clarity, focus and sound reason. She could not permit this.

"You came here looking for me."

His statement stopped her in her tracks and her mouth opened to launch a reflexive denial. A blatant lie.

He countered by taking several steps forward, forcing her behind the towering hedgerow lest he run her over with his powerful body. He stood inches from her. Her eyes were level with the top silver button of his waistcoat. They were now out of sight should any of the guests venture onto the terrace. Elizabeth tipped her head back to look into his face.

"Miss Smith, let us be honest with each other, shall we?" How he managed to coax and command in the same breath, she didn't know but his tone did both. "I have watched you…watch me…for many weeks now. You want this as much as I do." His silky voice was not for the weak or faint of heart. Ladies who easily succumbed to the vapors would have been a puddle at his feet by now.

Mesmerized, Elizabeth stood mute, inhaling his musky scent and fighting the weakness stealing over her limbs and making sawdust of her will.

His head began a slow descent giving her time enough to halt the whole thing before it went too far. "Would you like me to kiss you, Miss Smith?" He spoke softly and his voice lulled.

And for a moment she was lulled into believing that she had some control in this situation. That he had given that back to her.

"I-I do not make it a habit of kissing gentlemen I do not know—I mean at all." She didn't exactly push him away. She said precisely what a young lady of her rank ought to say but felt no satisfaction in it. Instead, it left her deprived, denied and wanting.

He chuckled softly. "Well there must be a first time for everything."

The viscount possessed a sensual allure so powerful and intoxicating it rendered her willing and eager to experience everything he offered. She leaned in, pure need driving her. But before the distance between their mouths could be bridged, he halted and pulled slightly back. "I will not take what you will not give freely. What do you want? You only have to tell me," he coaxed, his breath mingling with hers.

Elizabeth blinked several times before his handsome face came into focus.

Devil take him!

They had been doing perfectly well on the course he had set. Now, fully aware of the folly about to take place, she had no choice but to refuse him.

As if he sensed the turmoil roiling within her, he slid his hands around her waist, strong and possessive, so very familiar as if they hadn't spoken for the first time just that evening. "Will you deny us both?" With his words, the roughness of his voice and his proximity, her battered resistance collapsed in total defeat. She wanted this just as much if not more than he did; had wanted him in some fashion since she'd first laid eyes on him.

She shook her head and before she could take another wispy breath, his mouth was on hers, claiming her wholly.

Derek Creswell may be a lord by birth and a gentleman in appearances and comportment but his kiss told her there was nothing remotely proper about him. He was carnality at its most sinful.

This was no soft and tentative kiss of new lovers but one so sensual and hot, it reverberated through her right down to the soles of her feet. His tongue traced the softness of her lower lip before plunging inside to coax hers into a delicious love play.

Plowing her fingers through the thick vibrancy of his hair, Elizabeth twined her hands around his neck, and tipped her head back wanting nothing else but to submit and feed the hunger pulsing inside her. Her tongue worried his full bottom lip. A groan of pleasure rumbled from his chest as he took the kiss deeper, drugging her into mindlessness.

He pulled her closer at the same time she pressed for more contact. The hard thrust of his erection prodded heavily against her belly. A rush of moisture pooled between her thighs. Elizabeth briefly broke the kiss and let out a ragged moan. Clutching her backside firmly in his hands, Lord Creswell angled her hips so he could fit his erection where she was wet for him, ached to be filled by him. Pleasure stole her next breath and she gasped, wanting only to push against him without the encumbrance of skirts, petticoats and stays.

The click of a door was the same as spraying cold water on two particularly amorous dogs. They sprang apart, Elizabeth wrenching herself from the warmth of his arms, her breath coming in short halting pants, her body still thrumming with unquenched desire.

A young girl's tittered laughter filled the air. She was quickly hushed by a male voice and then all went silent but for the click of footsteps on the flagstone, until even that was no more. Fear of discovery made Elizabeth unwilling to chance a glance around their leafy shelter to ensure they were alone. Instead, she peered up at the viscount.

Except for the slight ruffling of his hair where her fingers had played, Lord Creswell did not appear all that affected by the kiss. But a look down revealed his erection straining against his black trousers.

She'd felt *that* pressed against her but the visual evidence of his arousal heightened her own.

"I should not have permitted you to kiss me like that."

"Then *how* should you have permitted me to kiss you?" he asked smiling. "Or perhaps the better question would be *where*." His gaze dropped suggestively to her breasts and then drifted lower. And lower still.

Dear Lord, he can't mean he would ever put his mouth there. The thought should have repulsed her but the heaviness at her center returned anew, growing slick under his heavy-lidded gaze.

"I didn't mean for you to kiss me at all," she said, her face fiery hot with embarrassment. What she spoke was the truth. She hadn't followed him out here to encourage much less participate in him taking such liberties. She'd wanted to meet him face-to-face and finally satisfy the curiosity about him she had harbored for six long years.

"Is that so? Well, I look forward to our next...meeting." He spoke softly and smiled almost gently, as if he was privy to something she was not.

Perhaps thoughts of all the things he wanted—intended to do with her.

Her faced burned. "I should go back. Missy must be wondering where I've got to." She hesitated, waiting but unsure of what. Certainly not to see if he'd try to convince her to remain where they could share more of those mind-drugging kisses. Her wanton response spoke for itself.

"I will not keep you then." He sketched a bow.

It was for the best.

"It probably would not be wise if we returned together. I will use the entrance on the side. Rutherford keeps that door open for these affairs. If you like, I shall go first." He lifted his brow in question, now all gallantry and polished composure.

Elizabeth agreed with a little nod and watched as he disappeared, silent and sure-footed, into the moonless night. When she heard the last of his retreat, she turned on her heel, dashed a quick glance around before making her way toward the French doors.

And then another voice emerged from the dark. "Why, Miss Smith, what a surprise."

CHAPTER THREE

At the sound of the nasally voice of Lady Danvers, Elizabeth immediately went as still as prey sensing danger. Instinct told her not to turn around, but to run and hide.

But she knew she couldn't outrun the reach of the dowager's influence and hiding would merely bring out the gossip hounds, who could sniff out a brewing scandal in their sleep.

Perhaps Lady Danvers hadn't witnessed anything untoward and thereby worthy of gossip, malicious or otherwise. Perhaps she was merely stopping her to exchange pleasantries. A perfectly lovely fantasy.

With a smile fixed in place, Elizabeth turned to confront the danger head on.

Oh Lud! Lady Danvers' presence would have been bad enough, but to add to Elizabeth's growing dismay, at her side stood Mrs. Abernathy, one of her mother's oldest and dearest friend. Her raised brow and tight lips conveyed a mixture of shock and concern.

What on earth was she doing here? Her mother had mentioned her friend would be visiting with her niece in London for a spell in the summer but had never mentioned an acquaintance with her cousin Missy or James.

"Who was that with you?" Lady Danvers demanded, her voice ringing out haughty and shrill. Her eyes, a shade of blue not heralded by the poets, flashed triumphantly behind a pair of gold-rimmed glasses.

When Elizabeth didn't immediately respond—for she could not think of one face saving thing to say—the dowager flicked a gloved hand at her as she made a coarse inspection of her from head to hem and then back up again. "You should be ashamed of yourself. I realize this is your first Season, but in London society, country girls are expected to comport themselves better than barn felines. Loose morals have no place here."

Elizabeth would have preferred to be cross-examined before the magistrate than suffer the dowager's dressing down. Her world was crumbling down around her and she could do little to stop the destruction.

Opposite of the Dowager Countess of Danvers in every possible way with her small-boned frame and impeccable manners, Mrs. Abernathy appeared unwilling to convict Elizabeth without a fair hearing. "Lady Danvers, I'm sure you are mistaken. I have known Elizabeth since she was a babe. If you would give the poor girl a chance, I'm quite certain she has a perfectly logical explanation."

Elizabeth could have kissed her, the dear woman. Mrs. Abernathy had always had a fondness for her and her sisters, bringing them treats on every visit with her mother.

"What possible explanation could there possibly be?

It's quite obvious they were doing a sight more than flower gazing. And don't you try to protect her. You heard their goings on as clearly as I did." The dowager folded fleshy arms across her ample breasts, refusing to budge an inch as she stood set to be jury and judge while wielding her executioner's sword like she'd been going so all her seventy odd years.

Elizabeth met Lady Danvers' disapproving glower without flinching. The Dowager Countess of Danvers was a formidable force in society, her influence wide reaching and much sought after. An unfavorable word from her lips would spell certain disaster for someone in Elizabeth's position.

Anger began a slow burn at the woman's arrogance.

What possible explanation indeed.

But Elizabeth wasn't addled in the brain as to respond the way she wanted—the way she ought to—fully understanding the ways of London society. A healthy dose of fear settled in the pit of her stomach.

Think, think, think.

She must tell the blasted woman something before the gossip wheels began to turn in earnest and at record breaking speeds. If the dowager countess had her way, Elizabeth and the Smith name would be dirt before the evening closed.

"My sincerest apologies, my lady, if my behavior has been indiscreet. But in my excitement, I acted out of character." Where she was going with this, Elizabeth hadn't the faintest idea, but Mrs. Abernathy's brown eyes widened and Lady Danvers gave a succinct nod, urging her to proceed. She now had their most focused attention.

"It's not to be announced until the end of the Season, but given what you heard, I shall tell you. I would hate it if you walked away thinking the worst of me."

Elizabeth drew in a deep breath and threw herself at the mercy of an uncertain fate. "The gentleman had just asked me to marry him. I am betrothed—or at least I shall before the end of the Season." Which gave her four weeks to perform that minor miracle.

A delighted smile, stretched across Mrs. Abernathy's face. "Oh my dear girl, that is wonderful. My, your mother never said of word of it to me." She clapped her hands together in girlish glee.

However, the dowager wasn't so easily fooled. She directed a level stare at Elizabeth that made her want to squirm. Acting was not one of Elizabeth's talents but with her future resting in the hands of an unyielding and austere Lady Danvers, she summoned up every bit of ingenuity she possessed—which did not account to much—and smiled a foolish, giddy smile of a young woman with stars in her eyes and love in her heart.

"And to *whom* are you betrothed?" the countess asked.

"Unfortunately, I cannot say until the gentleman receives the blessing of my father. Which my father will grant, of course, as the gentleman is titled," she added quickly, willing to say anything to remove the skepticism from the dowager's eyes.

Lady Danvers glanced at Mrs. Abernathy before

turning back to her. "A peer you say?" She spoke with enough doubt in her tone to offend.

The witch!

Although truthfully, Elizabeth acknowledged that before her father inherited his title, there was more a likelihood that money would fall from the sky than her marrying even a sir. But now it was indeed possible, especially with the one thousand pounds her father had settled on her.

Elizabeth drew back her shoulders and stiffened her spine. "Yes, my lady, a lord."

In response, the dowager raised one over-plucked eyebrow and gave a soft, harrumph before saying, "I will be expecting an introduction before you go announcing it to all of London."

If the woman had requested she deliver her the moon on a platter, Elizabeth would have gladly promised to do just that. But since thankfully, the dowager hadn't asked the impossible, Elizabeth just nodded vigorously. "You will be the first to know, that I promise."

"Make certain you do." The unspoken threat of revealing all the dowager had heard and seen tonight all over London simmered between them. "And do make yourself presentable before you go back inside. It shan't take a genius to guess what you have been up to."

Elizabeth acknowledged Mrs. Abernathy with a grateful smile, performed an ingratiating curtsey toward the dowager before hastily taking her leave, pondering how precisely she was going to get herself out of this mess.

~*~*~

After slipping back inside, Elizabeth was met by Missy. She attempted to excuse herself from the remainder of the ball pleading a headache but her cousin insisted they speak privately because she knew something was troubling her. As Elizabeth knew Missy would ruthlessly wear her down with her compassion and concern, she'd acquiesced without another word and led Missy to her bedchamber.

Five minutes later, Missy paced the carpeted floor at the foot of the bed, her slender fingers twirling a lock of chestnut hair she'd pulled from the pins securing it into an elegant coiffure, her smooth brow furrowed in fierce concentration.

"Well, I would definitely say you have managed to get yourself into quite a bind," Missy stated after a lengthy silence that followed Elizabeth's recount of the evening's events.

At least she hadn't told her how utterly thoughtless and foolish she'd been to have put herself in such a situation. Elizabeth had already berated herself up one side of Hyde Park and down the other.

"What am I to do?" she asked, doing her best to tamp down a wave of panic that seemed to ebb and flow depending on who, the viscount or the dowager, her thoughts centered upon.

Her cousin's expression immediately became contrite. Holding out her hand, she motioned Elizabeth to the large canopy bed. "Come, sit down. You look like a bundle of nerves. Don't fret so. All will be well, I promise."

Missy angled toward her once they were seated on the edge of the bed and looked Elizabeth in the eye. "Lord Creswell *must* marry you. I can see no other way."

Difficult as it was, Elizabeth had to face the truth of her words. And that wasn't to say she herself abhorred the thought. Her distress stemmed from the unfortunate circumstances and her one glaring omission. She had to tell him who she was.

"He is going to be angry."

Missy's back went straight as a board and a steely glint entered her blue-gray eyes. "Then he should have been more circumspect in his dealings with you," she said her voice cooling several degrees.

As much as Missy admired the viscount, Elizabeth knew her cousin would have no problem taking him on to defend her honor. Elizabeth dropped her gaze to her lap. Never had she felt so unworthy of such unstinting loyalty.

"I will speak with James tomorrow, you best get some sleep."

Elizabeth's face blistered with heat. Good Lord, what would he think of her? And worse yet, what would he do? "James will not-not—"

Missy's countenance softened and a teasing smile transformed her beautiful face to nothing short of breathtaking. "Don't worry, my dear, my husband is not a violent man. Moreover, he is terribly fond of Lord Creswell, as are we all."

"Oh no, I didn't mean—"

The soft lilting sound of Missy's laughter cut off Elizabeth's stricken protest. "Be assured, James will know precisely how to handle this situation. He's a very gifted arbitrator. Jason and Jessica are as malleable as clay in his hands," she said, speaking of her and James's two-year-old twins.

Elizabeth smiled faintly. She could well imagine. The earl had that kind of effect on people.

"But I don't want him to be forced to marry me if he is opposed."

"The viscount should consider himself very fortunate to have you as his wife."

Now would be the time to tell Missy about the less than amiable past they shared, but after seeing the hope and confidence in her cousin's eyes, Elizabeth couldn't bring herself to heap yet another bit of misery upon her tonight. Perhaps, when the morning dawned clear and bright, her future wouldn't appear quite so miserable and gray.

Gray skies and a misty rain greeted the morning. Derek didn't so much mind the gloomy weather for he hadn't any pressing plans that required him to leave his residence that day.

He was taking breakfast in the dining room when he heard the doorbell chime. Surprised, he shot a glance at the cherry, long-case clock by the far wall. Nine o'clock. Like many of his peers, he owned a well-appointed flat in Mayfair, but he did not normally receive callers before noon. On Sundays, no one called.

A minute later his manservant entered and inquired if he was in for Lord Alex Cartwright and Lord Windmere.

Curious but not alarmed, he instructed Paulson to have the men await him in the drawing room.

When he joined them, ten minutes later, Rutherford prowled the room. Cartwright stood in front of a narrow paned window that stretched the length of wall, his back to him, hands thrust deep into his trouser pockets as he looked out into small yard at the back. Both men turned at his entry.

Taking in the grim set of Cartwright's mouth and a somber Lord Windmere, Derek immediately evinced this wasn't to be a pleasure call.

"Good morning, gentlemen. I can see from your expressions you aren't here for the want of my company." Derek smiled in an attempt to ease the sudden tension in the room. Surely whatever the news, it couldn't be all that bad.

Cartwright shook his head, a move that held suppressed fury. "You couldn't just leave well enough alone could you? Damn it man, why couldn't you leave *her* alone when I expressly told you she isn't the type to dally with."

Bloody hell, they obviously knew about the kiss. But how? Miss Smith hadn't seemed the type to run and tell tales the moment his back was turned.

While Derek grappled with just how he should respond, Rutherford stalked toward him, his footsteps muffled by the rug underfoot. He looked menacing and severe. He halted in front of him.

Was he sizing him up? He and Rutherford were approximately the same height, an inch above six feet, and possessed similar frames. In a fight, neither would have an innate advantage.

"You *must* marry her," the earl said evenly.

What the devil had she told them?

"She's demanding I marry her because I kissed her?"

"Your embrace with Miss Smith did not go unobserved," Cartwright practically growled from behind Rutherford.

"Observed by whom?" Derek would not begin to panic just yet. Things may not be looking altogether rosy but surely they couldn't have already reached the catastrophic stage.

"At present, Lady Danvers doesn't know it was you with Miss Smith in the garden," Rutherford said grimly. "Despite her advancing years, her hearing is still as sharp as ever and it would appear you failed to keep your goings on strictly between Miss Smith and yourself. I don't believe I need to tell you how much this has distressed my wife."

Derek suppressed the groan that had built up in his

throat and the string of curses that sprang to his lips. The whole bloody thing was a mess.

While he admitted Elizabeth Smith heated his blood like no woman had in quite some time, that didn't mean he wanted to take her as his wife. To be forced to do so was even worse.

"I don't even know the woman." It was a weak argument but was all he had to offer.

"Well it appears you've received enough intimate knowledge of her to see her ruined." Cartwright ran his hand through his hair. "In any case, whether you know her sufficiently or not, you have to marry. She's in this fix because of you."

Like hell she is!

"I'll have you know, she was the one who followed me out to the garden. She was the one who sought me out. She is—" Derek broke off.

She'd set out to trap him.

Following him out to the garden. Crashing into him. Although, he'd known she had deliberately sought him out, he hadn't known how far she intended to take it. She must have known the dowager had been there, ears primed to hear all Miss Smith had set in motion.

The last time he'd had to deal with a female this treacherous and conniving, it had cost his father one thousand pounds to avoid the threat of a scandal. What would this one cost him today? His freedom?

"I did not pursue her. She pursued me."

"Whether she pursued you or you pursued her is

irrelevant. What matters is that you have a duty to her now. She is my wife's cousin and under our care while she resides with us." It was clear Rutherford would not countenance a refusal, his voice firm and final.

The unwelcome and unfamiliar feeling of helplessness made his limbs feel heavy and useless. He'd prided himself as being a man who solved problems, a man who remained level-headed in trying situations. At the moment, he felt as if he'd been knocked sideways and then pushed into a corner as the walls closed in around him.

Without saying a word, he crossed the room, picked up a glass tumbler from the sideboard and poured himself two fingers of whiskey. He downed it like a man who'd walked the length of the Sahara Desert without a drop of water. The burn in his throat remained when he turned back to face Rutherford and Cartwright.

"So where am I to find my dearest betrothed?"

33

CHAPTER FOUR

As good as her word, Missy had immediately informed her husband of the situation. Precisely what had occurred thereafter, Elizabeth wasn't certain. No doubt it entailed a talk with the viscount, and it appeared the earl had wasted no time about it because Lord Creswell arrived at the house just before midday the following day requesting an audience with her.

With more than a little reluctance, Elizabeth entered the morning room. The windows were abundant there, permitting lots of natural light. Truth be told, she was terrified. Her terror grew along with an engulfing dismay when he turned from the window to acknowledge her.

Her mind went blank for an instant. Her breath hitched at the sight of him. She had only seen him in his evening black and whites. She hadn't imagined less formal clothes would come close to doing him—his body—justice. She was wrong.

Clad in tan trousers, a cream waistcoat piped around the hem and collar and a sage single-breasted jacket, the term dashing was too staid a word to describe the viscount. Everything about him was male; his broad shoulders, the breadth of his chest, the sheer strength of him that one didn't need to witness to know he possessed in abundance.

While she tried not to be obvious in her admiration, he watched her, still and silent. Elizabeth had never been on the receiving end of a stare like the one he submitted her to. His attire may have consisted of warm soothing neutrals, but his eyes—said to be mirrors to the soul— were the cold of icebergs and north England winters.

Elizabeth shivered feeling his glacial freeze to the very marrow of her bones.

How things had changed since they'd kissed. Then, his attention had excited her, had brought out the wanton in her. Today, he indicated with just one look how much he despised her.

"Be honest, you followed me out onto the terrace did you not?" he said, cutting to the quick without even the pleasantry of a greeting.

Last night the fact had amused him. Today he intended to force an admission from her so he could bludgeon her with it.

It wouldn't do her any good to lie. But she certainly wouldn't confirm it with words.

He moved with an unhurried grace and crossed the room to her. His half foot height advantage seemed more so when he halted an arm length from her, no longer allowing her clarity of mind his distance had offered. He looked down at her, his mouth twisted in scorn. "Come now," he jeered softly. "Admit that you orchestrated the whole production—the meeting, the kiss and Lady

Danvers' timely presence."

Elizabeth shook her head emphatically. The latter two things he'd enumerated with such mocking disdain she would not accept the blame for. "My lord, you are forgetting one important fact, it was you who kissed me."

He emitted a dark laugh. He was not amused. "I am a man. Who was I not to succumb after being barraged by the signals you've been sending me the past month. Every time I turned around, there you were peeping at me with that come hither look in your eyes. But you were cleverer than most, never approaching because you knew that would pique my interest even more."

Her? Set out to beguile a man?

Good Lord, if he knew her the slightest bit, he'd know she hadn't the faintest notion of how to play those sorts of flirtatious games. If she was guilty of anything, it was the crime of finding him handsome and captivating—much to her cost.

"You made your interest obvious from the start. At all those balls and soirees, I could *feel* your gaze upon me. When I looked, you would look away. God, you certainly had me fooled. I actually believed you were an innocent, too shy to look at me direct. I convinced myself I should leave you alone, that you were too well-bred for a dalliance. But even then you'd already set your sights to loftier heights. Not a mistress, you wanted to be my wife."

"You could not be more wrong." Yes, he had his charms but she was not *that* desperate to find a husband. Even one who would undoubtedly be every girl's dream.

36

His nostrils flared and a dull shade of red slashed his cheekbones. He continued as if she hadn't spoken, his voice low and fierce. "I will not be forced into marriage. I certainly won't be forced into a marriage with you."

Elizabeth couldn't help an inward flinch. His words stung. Did he think she had no pride? Not the tiniest bit of self-respect as to thrust herself upon a man who made it so obvious how much he didn't want her?

Pride saved her from being thrown against the rocks at his disavowal. "This isn't what I wanted," she said in a firm voice refusing to crumble beneath the storm of his accusations. "But the truth of it is, I have very little choice in the matter. The damage a scandal like this would do to my family would be irreparable. I have a younger sister who will debut in two years. I do not have the luxury of thinking just of myself." That she'd realized during a fitful night of sleep. As much as she didn't want to force a marriage if he opposed it, the reality of her situation begged to differ.

Lord Creswell straightened to his full rather intimidating height so he could, no doubt, look down his nose even further at her.

"So you don't want this marriage any more than I? I would think that places us on the same side of this divide."

"Unfortunately, what either of us wants is immaterial. We both have our families to consider. I hear you also have a younger sister. Think of what a scandal could cost her."

His jaw tightened as if she'd struck a sore point. "Do you realize what it will cost me to marry a woman against my will and better judgment?"

"And do you know how it will affect me to marry a man who thinks so ill of me? I no more relish the prospect than you." She'd known he would be angry but hadn't been prepared for his vehemence. And it would only get worse...

"Yes, you may not relish it, but you will gladly take on the title of viscountess and all that goes with it."

"I have no need of your money." Of course he would cast her in the role of the gold-digger. "And although it may seem very gauche and naïve of me, I planned to marry for love."

For a long moment he didn't speak, merely watched her, his eyes intense and more green than blue. His expression was wiped clean of mockery and disdain, now an inscrutable mask. "Miss Smith, I do hope you're sure about this course on which you are about to embark. I am a man who does not like being taken for a fool."

Tell him. Tell him now.

Elizabeth knew she should heed the voice in her head urging her to be done with it, tell him everything. But in the face of his anger, his contempt, her courage failed her. If he was this furious now, she couldn't imagine the full extent of his fury if she told him before he had an opportunity to calm down, which given his reaction, would require days.

Yes, it would be best to allow him to get over his

initial bout of anger. Surely when he got to know her, he'd see that she wasn't capable of the deceit he'd accused her of. She would try to win him over, smooth the forbidding lines bracketing his mouth and furrowing his brows.

"I did not set out to trap you into marriage." She whispered the weary refrain at a loss of what else to say. "This entire situation is just as painful to me as it obviously is to you."

Some indiscernible emotion flashed in Lord Creswell's eyes. Resignation? It was hard to tell, he appeared to be able to mask his emotions at will.

"I am in an untenable position. I am damned no matter which path I take. I will be vilified should I not marry you and my family will be forced to endure the scandal. Should I marry you, it won't be of my own accord. At the very least, I assumed I'd be at liberty to choose my own wife." Much of the anger had dissipated from his voice.

"Obviously, this situation isn't ideal, but I hope we can make the best of it." Given the kiss that had landed them in their current predicament, they would be compatible in at least one area of their marriage.

Just the thought of the kiss made her warm all over. His gaze lowered in a slow perusal of her body and his eyes darkened as if in that moment, they shared the same thought and reaction to it. In the same leisurely pace, he tracked his way back up to her face. And lingered on her mouth.

"You did not set out to trap me?" There was no accusation in his voice, just a genuine desire for the truth.

That she could give him. "You have my word, Lord Creswell, that I did not set out to trap you."

He continued to stare at her and like a seedling struggling to take root in unruly soil with scant little water, something in that look acted upon her like a drenching rain. Hope flickered in her heart. After a grievously long silence, he appeared to accept his fate and acquiesced with a curt nod of his head. His words confirmed it. "I cannot marry a woman I do not know. I suggest we spend some time getting better acquainted."

Well, perhaps not complete acceptance, but close enough.

Elizabeth was nearly light-headed with relief and giddy with anticipation. It would work out. It had to work out. As she nodded, she could barely believe this man standing in front of her might—would one day be her husband. *Hers.* She would have the right to kiss those lips, caress that chest and touch those muscled shoulders. Her gaze followed the trail of her thoughts.

"But of course we must become properly acquainted," she agreed, pulling her thoughts back to the conversation at hand. Nervously, she ran the tip of her tongue over her bottom lip.

Lord Creswell tracked the movement with a searing gaze. Abruptly, he cleared his throat and shot a glance at the clock on the fireplace mantel.

"I have taken up enough of your morning. I will call on the morrow. Good day, Miss Smith."

"Good day, Lord Creswell," she said, her voice hardly

loud enough to be heard.

With that, he gave a nod and went on his way.

This didn't precisely put her in the clear. Elizabeth was well aware of that. There was another hurdle yet to clear. And to dull the impact the truth of their past connection would have—a connection she now resented for it stood in the way of her future happiness—she knew she *had* to get him to care for her.

Quite literally, she would have to wage a war of seduction. But not seduction in its most commonly used context. Although it would be far easier to get him into her bed but that wouldn't be enough to sustain of happy marriage. At least not 'til death do they part. No, she'd seduce him without the use of her body and at the same time capture his heart.

CHAPTER FIVE

By midmorning the next day, unseasonably cold temperatures had Londoners dragging out wool pelisses and heavy greatcoats. That the air remained dry was the day's one saving grace.

Derek observed Miss Smith from across his barouche. She looked good. Better than good if one admired silky skin, red lips that begged to be kissed and a figure that curved in and out in all the right places. He resented her; resented that a wave of lust had all but assaulted him when he'd arrived at Laurel House to collect her for their morning drive. And had yet to abate.

He could detect no yield to her spine as she sat, hands clasped tightly on her lap buried in the voluminous folds of her peach and gray skirts. She'd looked at him once, very briefly, then proceeded to focus all her attention on trying not to look at him. She was currently studying the interior with greater a scrutiny than he'd given it upon its purchase.

Derek tapped the roof twice. The carriage immediately jolted into motion.

She looked at him then, eyes wide as if startled that they were moving as conveyances often do.

"You are well?" he asked courteously.

Her mouth curved in a strained smile. "I suppose I am well given the circumstances."

Her chin quivered the barest little bit. Fright? Nerves? Perhaps a bit of both. Her hands had not been still since she'd taken her seat.

Lord above, he didn't want to incite fear in her. He wanted—wanted his life back to the way it was before he'd kissed her. But he wanted the memory of the kiss. He wanted to kiss her again. Hell, he wanted to do a sight more than that. But he couldn't have both.

"And you?"

Derek wondered if she really cared or was simply being polite. He wondered how she'd react if he told her precisely where his thoughts lay. He decided to ignore her question altogether and asked instead, "Miss Smith, I imagine that if I was able to arrange things so that you could retain your reputation without us being forced to wed, you would be relieved?"

Her answer should have been an instantaneous, *But of course, my lord.* But that was not how she reacted. Her shoulders jumped and her eyes were now two enormous orbs in her sweet oval face.

She recovered quickly but had it been from shock or something else? Disappointment? He mulled over which reaction he preferred.

"But of course, my lord," she replied.

Derek forced a smile. *Of course.* Not the response of a woman trapped in circumstances under which she had no control and she would gladly extricate herself from if she could.

"Although, I can't imagine how you would manage it. While I'm positive Mrs. Abernathy would never breathe a word of it to anyone, the dowager is another matter. I believe she's eager to see me ruined."

She adjusted her bonnet as if it rested uncomfortably on her head. "Why, have you figured a way out?"

"No." Although he did have his man of business working on something. But it would take a bit of time. Ten days he'd been told.

She looked down at her hands tightly clasped in her lap and now her brim obscured her face from view. He wished she'd take the damn thing off.

She laughed but it was a fragile and thin sound. "Am I that bad a prospect?"

Derek swallowed hard and shifted in his seat. For a reason he couldn't fathom, he wanted to put a smile back on her face. To see the same light passion had ignited in her eyes those moments in the garden.

"That's not it at all. I'm certain there are more men than I could count who would be proud to call you their wife." It was only after he'd uttered the words and tested them in his ears that he realized what ill a fit it was, well-meaning though they were.

"But not you." she said, but looked up at him as if expecting an answer.

Her gaze struck him. Those eyes. Had he ever seen a color quite like it? Brown liberally peppered with light

44

flecks of gold. Not one dash of green in them. Beautiful. While he may not want her as his wife, he could imagine other positions he'd enjoy having her in. He grew hard, his cock responding to his thought as if it'd received a physical stroke.

"I don't know you well enough to say." His voice was graveled in large part because he couldn't control his reaction to her.

"That didn't prevent you from kissing me."

"Miss Smith, if I were to wed every woman I kissed, I would have been a husband many times over." He would have been wed at the age of twelve.

A soft blush suffused her face and she fell silent.

As passionate as her response to him had been, Derek could clearly see she was an innocent. A virgin. And virgins wanted everything proper: the courtship, the wedding, and the bedding. Everything in its rightful order.

If everything went as he firmly expected it would, there would be no need for a marriage. Which meant there wouldn't be a bedding. His cock twitched as if in protest. But if circumstances concluded they did have to wed, he wondered if she had any real comprehension of just what she was letting herself in for. He was a man of healthy sexual appetites and in regard to her, his appetite had grown. What would she say to being kept in bed for days, for that's how long it might take to sate his initial hunger for her.

"And you are quite certain you have no objection to marrying me?" This wasn't a fishing expedition, more a subtle warning.

She laughed and the sound caught him square in the gut. The word delightful came to mind.

"You ask as if you're some horrible ogre, which you certainly are not."

Derek sat back against the squab as he tried to decipher the puzzle that was Elizabeth Smith. She was forthright...to a point. But still so naïve when it came to men.

Had she indeed set out to trap him? He'd pondered that question all night. The part of him that wanted to shag her senseless was inclined to believe her. But the other part of him had long decided that most women couldn't be trusted.

If his man returned with the information Derek needed, the plan could only work if Miss Smith didn't sow the seeds of scandal herself. Given her recent response, he couldn't trust that she would. What he needed was that she find him less than desirous as a prospective husband.

"You do realize that as your husband I will have certain rights?"

Finely arched brows met above the bridge of her nose. She appeared to puzzle over his question. Realization dawned swiftly, her eyes going wide, her lips parting in a silent *oh*.

Derek abandoned his seat and took the one next to her, which caused her to slide across the leather seat and practically hug the door.

"Watch that you don't tumble from the carriage," he

said in mock warning. "Come closer, there is enough room for both of us here. Remember, you will have to suffer me much much closer."

Miss Smith eased from the door to turn wary eyes to him. "I'm well aware of what will be required of me in marriage."

Derek lifted a brow. "Then tell me. I am particularly interested as it relates to our marriage bed."

Elizabeth let out a gasp. A glance at him revealed even, white teeth between a crooked smile and hooded eyes. But he didn't appear the least bit amused. His direct stare demanded an answer.

"Pardon?" She couldn't help the squeak in her voice as the word emerged.

"Was I faulty in my speech?"

Elizabeth marveled that he could keep his expression deadpan.

"I would like you to tell me what it is you must do in the marriage bed."

His question was-was so beyond the realm of social acceptability when it came to conversations between an unmarried man and woman, Elizabeth would not be surprised if the Gentleman's Handbook didn't fall from the sky and knock him senseless.

"My lord, I have no intention—"

"I hope you will not lie under me as stiff as a board. I like my bed partners engaged and enthusiastic."

Elizabeth could only stare at him in mute horror. She'd

admit to being only slightly aroused.

His mouth curved but it could not be considered a smile. He made a soft clicking sound with his tongue. "If I'm to be your husband, Miss Smith, you will have to grow accustomed to my frankness."

Before she could so much as utter a word, he closed the distance between them with a swiftness that transfixed her.

"You must also grow accustomed to my touch, to my kiss," he murmured, sharing a breath with her before he took her mouth in a kiss that stole the air from her lungs.

Dizzying was the only way she could describe the touch of his lips on hers, the skillful way his tongue stroked hers. For several seconds she did nothing but feel while another kind of heat warmed her from inside to out.

In no time at all, he released her from the shackles of her pelisse, freeing him to stroke her from her waist to just below her breast. Thoughts of stopping him came and then vanished on a wave of pleasure too intense to be denied.

Dropping her head back against the squab, Elizabeth returned his kiss with a reckless abandonment that surprised her. With his facile tongue, he showed her how to use hers with the same devastating effect. She mimicked his slow thrust, their tongues entwined, sliding, stroking. He emitted a groan that sent a myriad of tremors through her body as he dragged her onto his lap.

His hand took another tortuous tour of her torso until it once again rested lightly beneath her aching breasts. She wanted him to touch her there. Her back bowed, her breast offered up to him like a banquet.

"Tell me what you want," he urged, breaking the kiss.

Even with lust fogging her senses, Elizabeth could not. She could never bring herself to be so bold.

At her pause, his hand traveled up and stroked her hard nipple through the silk of her day dress.

"Yes," she said, panting.

He kissed that so sensitive place where her neck joined her shoulder. His lips then went on to explore her jaw, her chin, her cheeks until he reached her bottom lip where he took her mouth in one last deep and drugging kiss. Slowly, as if trying not to startle her, he set her from his lap, straightened her bonnet that had become askew in their embrace and took his place on the seat facing her.

"We have arrived," he said in way of explanation.

Elizabeth immediately pushed aside the curtain of the window closest and saw they were back at her cousin's residence. She couldn't even remember if they'd actually gone to the park. But yet here they were.

Derek did not deal well with thwarted desire. But as he hadn't been about to take the delectable Miss Smith in the carriage, that was precisely the state he found himself in when they returned to the house. A footman met them at the door. In silence, they followed him into the foyer.

He turned to her. She had taken an inordinate interest in the marble floors, unable or unwilling—he wasn't sure which—to meet his gaze. A hasty goodbye and mumbled excuses trailed in her wake as she escaped up the stairs, hands trembling, skirts flying.

She was shaken; completely unnerved by the intensity of their passion. She should be. The very same thing had given him reason to question whether he wanted a way out. The desire between them crackled and hissed like a fire that threatened to blaze out of control unless they fought to keep it contained.

But did he want it contained? He was even less certain he wanted all that passion unleashed on another man.

Another man? Is that how he now saw her potential suitors in the span of only one day of actually meeting her?

"Lord Creswell, may I have a word before you leave?"

Ready to make his departure, Derek halted and turned, his hat and gloves still in hand. A glance behind him, revealed Millicent Rutherford, the Countess of Windmere, standing in the middle of the foyer. He'd thought her lovely when she'd come out six years before and after three years of marriage and two children, she was even lovelier, tall and slim with the most beautiful, expressive eyes. At the moment they appeared concerned.

"Lady Windmere," he said in greeting, and made his way toward her.

"I pray you had a pleasant drive?" she said, when he reached her side. They turned and as if by tacit agreement, entered the drawing room.

"I did."

"And things are well between you and Elizabeth?" A subtle, ladylike probe into his private affairs.

He gave a rueful smile. Her concern for her cousin was expected. No doubt Rutherford had told her his edict of marriage had been met with something less than joy.

"I wager we will muddle through this well enough." One way or another.

"You are a true gentleman. Thank you." Lady Windmere took his hand and gave it an affectionate squeeze. "Things have not been easy for Cousin Margaret these last several years. That's Elizabeth's mother. I don't know how she would handle such a scandal."

"Where is she from, your cousin?" he asked. He knew practically nothing of her except the taste of her lips, the firm softness of her breasts, how she felt pressed up against him.

"Penkridge. It's a tiny village in Staffordshire. I'm sure you've never heard of it."

Derek stilled. Not only had he heard of the town but he'd had cause to go there six winters ago. That's when the past rose up to sully the present. Margaret. That had been the name of the mother. The bank draft had been made out to Mr. Joseph Smith, a local solicitor of meager means and three daughters. He knew only the name of the eldest—the calamity had given him good cause to never forget it—Madeline.

"Her father, what is his occupation?" He strived to keep the urgency from his voice.

The countess shot him a surprised look. She knew him well enough to know he wasn't the sort to stand on ceremony and was a man who would never judge another by his station in life. "Cousin Joseph is a solicitor. But I don't believe he retained his practice since he came into the barony."

For several seconds Derek remained silent, schooling his features as he endeavored not to give any indication of how great an impact what she'd just revealed had on him.

He'd been duped, played for the veriest fool. And the irony did not escape him that he'd been nearly caught in the same trap he'd helped his brother escape years before.

Now the younger sister had him on the hooks and thought to reel him in with the ease of an accomplished fisherman. She told him she'd be ruined if he did not marry her, her family's name dragged through the gutter that was the *ton's* gossip mill.

Ruined. For a kiss.

By God, if she was to be ruined, it shouldn't be over a paltry kiss. No, he'd show her the true meaning of ruin.

CHAPTER SIX

The following day, when Lord Creswell asked her if she'd like to visit Kensington Gardens, Elizabeth was surprised. Flowers, trees and acres upon acres of lush greenery were not the sort of things she'd thought would interest him. But upon their arrival, Missy and James firmly in tow, she'd immediately understood why the viscount had chosen that particular venue.

This was the sort of public place that offered privacy in the midst of a thriving metropolitan city like London. It made one think of the country.

Large elms surrounded a picturesque flower garden directly in front of the palace where a good two dozen people strolled, the ladies holding their parasols in a death-like grip as if fearing mere word of the sun shining high in the sky would wreak havoc on their pristine white skin.

Elizabeth peeked up at the viscount. They'd separated from Missy and James a minute ago and he'd been excessively quiet, not that she knew him well enough to make the observation, but somehow she just *knew*.

"Are you, by any chance trying to read me, Miss Smith?" He spoke quietly enough to soothe a child to sleep or quite contrarily cause a woman to abandon every last one of her inhibitions to hear him speak to her again and again.

She did not have the luxury of abandoning anything. With her reputation hovering on the precipice of respectability, mistakes would not be afforded her. Lady Danvers had seen to that.

"You have been quiet. I was pondering at the cause." She could be frank about this.

The white of his teeth glinted like a pearl catching the ray of the sun as a smile tugged the corners of his mouth upward.

Elizabeth was immediately short of breath. She wanted to remove her gloves. It had grown overly warm in the past minute.

"And I was pondering the exact same thought about you."

He was right in that.

"So tell me, Miss Smith, where is it you hail from? Cartwright has told me your father recently came into a barony and this is your first Season."

Personal questions, as inevitable as her next shaky breath, but how forthcoming could she be with him without him guessing the truth? This was a minefield she had to cross with pinpoint precision. One wrong step…

"I live in Wilton."

They walked slowly, truly barely walking at all. The wide path meandered through towering Hawthorns and horse-chestnut trees. There were couples and children's giggles and excited cries off in the distance, all in their own secluded world.

As were they. Or so it seemed.

"Wilton you say? I've had cause to go there a time or two." He didn't expound on his statement and fearing further discussion on the subject would lead them down a far more dangerous path than the one they traversed today, Elizabeth was content to leave it at that.

"So tell me, Miss Smith, why did you allow me to kiss you if you weren't hoping to secure a good marriage for yourself?"

He asked it oh so casually, as insouciantly as if society hadn't been founded on certain moral codes and forms of address. She should have been offended. And she didn't know he *hadn't* meant to offend. There was something today, something different, in his piercing gaze, as if he were measuring her like a tailor did his clients, knowledgeable enough in the subject to accurately guess the breadth, width and length of the cut.

Had he meant to catch her off guard? Fray her with his candor.

"I'm certain you know the answer to that? Have you chanced upon a mirror of late? Has no woman before succumbed to your looks and charms? I certainly can't be the first and I very much doubt I shall be the last. Although, I shan't tolerate a faithless husband."

Such impertinence. But it was best she laid her expectations of marriage bare for him to ponder.

His black brows rose slowly. He stopped right there in

the middle of the path and observed her as if she was a puzzle he was trying to solve. And Lord above, he even did *that* in such a way that caused every nerve in her body to quiver as if touched.

It was difficult not to be aware of him in that very visceral, basic way, but with his penetrating stare, that awareness was ratcheted up several notches. She was cinched into her corset, her petticoats riffled between her silk walking dress. But for all the fine muslin and silk, she felt bare under his stare. Naked and wholly exposed.

"To look at you, I would never imagine you could be so...frank." He spoke softly, almost as if he'd inadvertently uttered his thoughts aloud. "Are you this frank about everything, I wonder."

It wasn't precisely a question, but the way he regarded her indicated he expected an answer.

"I suppose I am." Was that her voice, so small and timid-like? Half-truths did rather come out that way, didn't they?

"And fastidiously honest?"

Had he shot her with an arrow, the question couldn't have pierced her more. But she soldiered on. There would come a right time for that particular confession. Here and now was neither the time nor place.

"I would like to consider myself so." Which was not a lie. Up to this point in her life, she had been fastidiously honest. In any case, she hadn't lied to him. An omission wasn't precisely an untruth.

He resumed walking, his long legs encased in fine

navy wool, carried him easily and steadily down the path. The infinitesimal pause in his stride she presumed was for her benefit, so could catch up with him, which she did without thought.

With his attention focused directly in front, he offered her his profile. If she was a painter, she'd like nothing better than to paint him for he had one of those faces. His nose was perfectly shaped for his squared-jawed face; not too large or too small. And dare she even look at his mouth too long, her center would ache, the pulling sort that compelled a body to do something to either satisfy it or make it cease at once.

She was staring at him rather boldly now. There was nothing not to like about his face. Nothing.

Aware he was being intently observed, he angled a glance down at her, his eyebrow raised. As if he knew her thoughts and was thusly amused by them.

"Like what you see?"

A question only the most arrogant man would ask of a lady.

Elizabeth refused to blush, cooling her cheeks with the force of her will. "If I said that I do, would you think me too forward?"

The path rose to a gentle sloping hill. He didn't speak until they'd crested the top. The sun dappled the leaves with brilliant white light and skittered across his head making his hair take on a sheen that reminded Elizabeth of newly shined, black Hessian boots.

"Are you this frank with all the men you meet, Miss

Smith, or am I the exception? Should we marry, I would hate to think that my wife can be so easily led by a handsome face, some whispered words and she'd be fair taking for one and all."

Elizabeth came to a halt with the jarring suddenness of a wall going up directly in front of her. Her mouth sagged and an assaulted breath expulsed from her mouth. Although, he posed a question, there was no mistake it had been a warning. She took her time forming her response in her mind before speaking them aloud.

"By the same token, my lord, I too hope you aren't as easily led. Speaking for myself, I know I have kissed only one man...ever. And I have met my share of handsome gentlemen. Can you say the same? *Should* we marry—and it would appear you have some question that we shall—do I need to worry about you taking liberties in the gardens with every woman who strikes *your* fancy?"

Elizabeth had worked herself into a righteous indignation that had her chest falling and rising rapidly.

In the distance, a child's playful shriek rippled the air. The viscount waited until silence wafted over them before he replied, "*Touché*. And if it will put your mind at rest, I don't normally kiss women I don't know. And I've never done so at a ball—at least not since I was much younger. You mightn't think it, but I'm usually overly cautious in guarding my personal affairs."

And just like that, her anger died. "Yet you kissed me." The viscount had taken a big risk kissing her as he had. Which meant *something* did it not?

"Yes, I kissed you." His eyes were half-mast now as they focused on the very place he'd kissed. Her mouth.

But no, she couldn't permit it. This was her seduction not his. And by the look on his face, his would be carnal lust, scorching kisses and unadulterated passion. The nature of those very emotions would incinerate everything, pull the focus from where it ought to be, which was them getting to know each other.

"So tell me, my lord, what are you interests? Are you an avid hunter?" Lord, she hoped not. She quite despised it as pure sport, the shooting of helpless animals.

He lifted his gaze from her mouth and his own curved the barest little bit as he looked into her eyes. *I will drop the subject of the kiss...for now*, his smile seemed to say.

"No, I'm not a hunter. Gave my father palpitations when he realized it. I don't think he ever forgave me for it," he said, with a quiet chuckle.

His father had died three years ago. The news had filtered back to her parents in Penkridge, which was how she'd come by the knowledge. Her sympathies had immediately gone out to the viscount and she'd thought of him often in the following months, wondering how he was bearing his grief.

"No, I'd rather work with my hands."

She searched his expression for signs of mockery but found none.

"I make things out of wood. Carve them," he elaborated quickly.

Now this intrigued her. A man who was good with his

hands. In other ways.

Miss Smith was good. *Very good.* If her sister had even half her...charms, it was no wonder his brother had become so smitten with her. But with foresight came the ability to guard himself against whatever spell she was hoping to cast over him. Her interest in him was hardly genuine. She was playing a role the way she was no doubt instructed to play.

And why he'd even told her about the hobby he taken up as a boy, he didn't know. So very few of his friends knew of his love of carving.

"What sorts of things do you make?"

She was better than good; she could star in her very own play on Drury Lane. But he'd indulge her until he decided just what to do with her.

"Animals. Sometimes people if I find them interesting enough."

She smiled at that, a tiny dimple appearing at the corner of her mouth. He idly wondered what it would be like to kiss her there, taste the soft concave skin with his tongue. He could feel himself hardening, which annoyed him more than a little bit.

"What kind of wood do you use?"

"Lime."

"Why lime?"

Since she was making such a good show of it, he'd indulge her a little longer. "Because it is a soft wood, easy to work with and has very little grain."

She appeared genuinely pleased by the information as if digesting something of great value. "And are you very good?"

The breeze tangled with the ribbon of her bonnet, sending it rippling languidly over the brim. She batted it away with a gloved hand.

"Have you seen the Statue of David?" he asked.

"I've seen pictures in a book." She now looked suitably impressed.

"Well I'm not *that* good."

When she let out a burst of laughter, Derek realized how much he'd wanted to hear that sound. He loved the slight throatiness of her voice, the way her eyes danced and her shoulders shook. And her smile…captivated him.

"I would love to see your work one day." She held the errant red laced ribbon in her grasp to keep it out of her face as she stared up at him.

He stopped and led her a few feet to stand beneath a horse-chestnut tree whose knotted trunk was bigger than the rear wheels on his barouche. "Would you like some help with that?" he asked, pointing to her ribbon.

She pondered his question a moment too long. He slipped the ribbon from her motionless fingers and proceeded to tie it in a bow. When he was finished, she tipped her head up, her eyes wide watching him.

Her mouth looked plush and pink and meant to be kissed. His cock stirred urging him to do just that.

Panic flared briefly in her eyes as he lowered his head. She quickly dropped her head and took two steps back.

"Thank you," she said, her voice breathless, her face flushed and not from the heat of the day. He liked that he could do that to her.

"You want me to kiss you," he stated, not about to pretend that hadn't been his intent.

The color on her face deepened, spreading to wash the gentle jut of her collar bones and down to sweep over the expanse of creamy skin exposed by her square-shaped neckline. "I don't think that would be a good idea. We are in a public park."

Derek looked around briefly. "No one is about."

She buried her hand in the folds of her skirts and he saw her fingers moving restlessly over the ice blue silk material.

"What scares you more, Miss Smith, that I won't stop or that you won't want me to?"

Her head jerked sharply up and he saw the truth there in her wide eyes.

"I would never force myself on a woman."

If Lord Creswell had meant to reassure her, she remained anything but. He was correct, she had no fear of him. It was the emotions he stirred in her with so little effort.

Elizabeth blinked and shook her head in denial. "I never said any such thing."

Lord Creswell smiled. "Then it would seem I have my answer."

He moved with the swiftness of a snake striking, his

gloved hand firmly palming the nape of her neck and tipping her head up for his kiss in one clean motion. His mouth settled on hers gently coaxing, rubbing. Her lips parted instantly, her response as natural as breathing. His tongue plunged into the wet, warm caverns of her mouth with the single-minded purpose to conquer, possess, plunder.

All tenderness was gone and in its place was greed and the most basic sexual desire. Like a ferocious vortex, she felt it pulling her under buffeted by her needs and her own wants.

But she couldn't let this happen, not again. It was this same sort of reckless desire that had women wringing their hands in heartsick despair after the men took their fill and walked away without a glance, promises broken, leaving the women's left hand bereft of a ring. It had happened to Madeline and if she wasn't very careful, it would happen to her.

She broke the kiss with the inexorable press of her hands against his shoulders. He allowed her to push him away for it was the only way she could have managed it. For a moment he looked as if he was about to protest. He narrowed his gaze down at her.

Slowly, as if fearing any sudden movement on his part would cause her to bolt, he caught her arm in his and lifted it for inspection. Elizabeth had no idea what he was looking for but permitted him to turn it gently in his hand. Her gown had small capped sleeves and her gloves came to her wrist so there was a length of pale flesh to peruse and to touch.

"So soft," he whispered, lazily stroking her forearm with his index finger. "Whoever thought something this slim and fragile in appearance would have so much strength," he mused, his mouth twisted.

Not yet recovered from the sheer wonder of the kiss, Elizabeth's arm tingled every place he touched.

He ran the back of his gloved hand along the now prickled skin of her bicep. "Do you play croquet, Miss Smith?"

She shook her head both in bemusement and in response to the question.

"I will teach you soon. It would be a shame to waste this arm keeping gentlemen at bay."

He smiled, a banked irony glinting in his beautiful eyes. Lifting her arm, he watched her steadily as he placed a soft kiss on the vulnerable skin just above her glove. Her chest rose on a swift inhale of a startled breath. And then the heat swept in like an invading army making a mockery of all her good intentions

No sane person fell in love in the span of a single day. But she could feel herself taking a headlong plunge into some foreign emotion more heartfelt than a girlhood crush, leaving her vulnerable in a way she'd never been.

He released her with the same languid speed. He smiled but it wasn't a smile that reassured a woman intent on retaining her virginity until she was securely wed.

"Shall we find Lord and Lady Windmere?" He proffered his arm, his expression cryptic, his manners exquisite.

As Elizabeth took his arm, she had the distinct feeling she'd just relinquished more of herself to him than just her hand.

CHAPTER SEVEN

Elizabeth had very little experience with men, and none at all with a man like Lord Creswell. There was nothing tentative about him, not the vaguest sense of uncertainty in his words or actions. And who would have thought a man could be competent in everything? At least it appeared that way to her.

Last week, the viscount had taken her to the theatre where he'd shown a more than passing knowledge of Italian. He'd danced with her at three balls, and as she'd come to expect, few men could match his skill on the dance floor.

Yesterday, and as promised, he taught her to play croquet. His manner of teaching had reduced her will to resist him to ashes, his chest pressing lightly on her back, his hands enclosed over hers as he guided her swing of the mallet. His body was long and muscled. And hard everywhere.

Had Missy, Charlotte and Catherine not been in attendance, she was certain he would have kissed her. And she no doubt would have kissed him right back. It was a very fortunate thing they'd been chaperoned.

Today, they were taking afternoon tea in the parlor at

Laurel House, something they'd never done before. But the viscount had been busy most of the day, and had only an hour to visit with her since he would be busy again that evening. He would miss escorting her to Lady Summerville's supper party.

Lord Creswell helped himself to flaky French pastries from the serving tray.

"You seem very fond of Miss Foxworth. I believe you've danced with her at every ball we've attended." After the words were out of her mouth, Elizabeth furiously wished she could snatch them back and rephrase them so she didn't sound like a shrewish, jealous witch.

The viscount watched her, his expression inscrutable as he proceeded to consume the cherry tart.

To fill the lengthening silence, Elizabeth hastily took a gulp of her tea, nearly burning her tongue in the process. She returned the teacup to the saucer with clatter of porcelain against porcelain.

"I am very fond of Miss Foxworth," he agreed. "And I am fond of Lady Gertrude and Miss Roswell, both whom I also partner to dance when they are in attendance."

"I didn't mean to imply—"

"Miss Smith, I'm sure you've been beautiful all your life. However, most women are not graced with your extraordinary looks and therefore, are often ignored. I am fortunate to be in a position to aid where I can and more often than not, when I dance with my friends, other men will follow. Every woman should enjoy a full dance card at a ball, wouldn't you agree?"

Elizabeth nodded mutely for no words could adequately express what she was feeling at that precise moment.

For the past several weeks, she had been teetering on the precipice of love, but what she'd just heard from the viscount succeeded in nudging her over.

Derek had paid quite a hefty sum for the information he now had in his possession: dates, names, places. He could put a halt to this thing with Miss Smith today if he so desired. The marriage she'd schemed to get would never come to pass. That very fact should have pleased him.

To his shame, it did not.

And he blamed her for that. If she hadn't tried to tread in very same shoes that her sister had worn six years ago, she may have been the one he could see spending the rest of his days with. The woman he could see bearing his children. The woman he could have loved. But she would never be any of those things for she was who she was.

One would think her misdeeds would stop him from wanting her. Again, to his shame, it did not. And that angered him more than her deceit—this hold she had on him. Well today he was determined to break that hold once and for all.

Like the prior day, Miss Smith had invited Charlotte Rutherford and one of her ardent suitors, Baron Lawrence

Stanfield, to accompany them on their daily outing. Today they were visiting the British Museum. The four stood just inside the entrance of the building.

"Where shall we go first?" Miss Smith spoke to no one in particular as she surveyed the museum, her eyes round with wonder.

"Why don't we start with the King's Library?" Miss Rutherford suggested when it became apparent neither he nor Lord Stanfield would offer up any themselves.

Miss Smith looked at him and then at the baron. "If my lords are in agreement?"

Derek jerked his head in a nod. But after the museum, they had a house to see with neither Miss Rutherford nor Stanfield in tow. But that was something Miss Elizabeth Smith didn't know. At least not yet.

Just as they began their walk toward the first wing of the building, Cartwright—he recognized his friend's voice instantly—called out from behind.

Miss Rutherford froze, inhaled a sharp breath as color leeched from her face. She collected herself a heartbeat later, her shoulders pushed slightly back, her chin raised the barest fraction of an inch.

His friend wasted no time in making his way to them. They exchanged silent nods upon his approach. To the women he offered a deep bow with the overly polite greeting of, "Miss Smith, Miss Rutherford." The nod he directed at Stanfield was cold, a tenuous hold on civility.

"Miss Rutherford, Lady Windmere has received word that Lady Armstrong is about to deliver. We will be leaving for Devon within the hour. "

Miss Rutherford eyes rounded in a mixture of concern and excitement. "So soon? Oh, but yes of course."

"I will escort you home."

At this, Miss Rutherford sent the baron a concerned look, who appeared impervious to the exchange and the resulting effect. As if Cartwright didn't pose a threat to Miss Rutherford's affection. The notion was laughable.

"Lord Stanfield?" Miss Rutherford prompted.

"Oh, yes. Cartwright, I will escort Miss Rutherford home."

"My carriage is close by and I'm on my way there," Cartwright replied tersely.

"I will instruct my driver to take you home, Stanfield," Derek offered. The man certainly wasn't going to remain with them, not with Miss Rutherford rushing off to be there at the birth of Armstrong's first child. Stanfield could do nothing else but accept his offer unless he wished to hire a hackney home as they had all come together in Derek's carriage.

Stanfield gave a grudging nod and ten minutes later, the trio had departed.

Now blessedly alone with Miss Smith, Derek directed his full attention at her, his elbow crooked. She peered up at him, her eyes uncertain perhaps a little afraid. He suppressed a smile and asked graciously, "Shall we?"

"Di-did you have anything to do with that?" she asked after a pause, her hand resting lightly on his forearm.

Elizabeth was quite sure he had. It simply couldn't be a coincidence.

His frame shook with laughter, drawing her gaze up to his.

"Even I could not foresee the precise timing of Lady Armstrong's child readying itself to enter the world. Really, Miss Smith, you think too much of my abilities. Am I now a mystic? A sightseer?"

Elizabeth understood just how ridiculous she sounded, but she just knew he'd had a hand in this even if she could not say exactly how. She also knew she was in a heap of trouble. He had that look in his eyes. The same look that had kept her on edge these last two weeks. An unabashed want that mirrored her own.

From their first kiss, she had known this was how it would be between them, that razor sharp awareness and a hunger that grew with every word, every touch and every look exchanged. And now with Charlotte gone, Elizabeth would have to cope on her own. Be strong in spite of herself. Things did not look promising.

They toured the museum the next several hours, taking in the royal collection of books in the King's Library. They moved on to see the Rosetta Stone before concluding their visit with the statue of the Great Winged Bull. He impressed her with his superior knowledge, speaking with great authority on the subject of Egyptian hieroglyphs and various other topics.

She also discovered his love of reading was as great as her own. At that, some of her anxiety eased, Lord

Creswell conducting himself like a perfect gentleman. He was solicitous in his touch and respectful in his manner, never once stripping her bare with his gaze.

When they tumbled into the carriage in the early evening, Elizabeth had convinced herself she could trust him to keep his hands—and all parts of him—to himself.

The waning rays of the sun heralded dusk, shrouding the carriage in darkness. Lord Creswell sat across from her, his figure cast in a shadow of gray and black. Except to ask her if she'd enjoyed the visit, he remained silent. Which wouldn't have been all that bad had she not known he was watching her. She could feel it. And the same tension she'd fear would derail her efforts came back, humming in the air stronger than before.

Some minutes later, the barouche came to a halt beside a townhome; a red-brick edifice that soared three stories high.

"Why have we stopped here?" she asked. *Who lives here?*

"It's a property I've just purchased. I thought you'd like to see it, perhaps offer your thoughts. You will be residing here, after all," came his smooth reply.

Elizabeth peered out the window and then back at his shadowed face. If she couldn't see him, she couldn't read him and therefore wouldn't know whether to trust him. But a far more dire situation than that was she didn't trust herself.

"I would prefer we come back another time."
Coward.

No, simply self-preservation.

"Really, Miss Smith, does the thought of being alone with me fill you with such fear? In any case, the groom needs to tend the horses. Come now," he cajoled, "I promise I won't bite." His tone did nothing to reassure her. He sounded sensually sinister if two such words could be put together in that way.

Elizabeth collected herself, pushing back her shoulders and swallowing hard. No one could mistake his statement for anything less than the challenge it was. She could do this. She wasn't so weak, so completely lacking in control.

But then, one could expect to resist only so much temptation and Lord Derek Creswell was undeniably temptation incarnate.

"Ten minutes." That should be time enough to take a quick tour of the house but surely not time enough for anything grievously untoward to occur.

"As you wish."

She could hear the smile in his voice and her apprehension mounted anew.

The first thing Elizabeth noticed upon entering the house was that they hadn't been greeted by a servant; not a butler or a footman or even a housekeeper. The sound of silence echoed throughout the empty halls.

"Where are the servants?"

"I haven't staffed the house as yet. I wanted your opinion of it as the sale is not yet final."

Had he not just told her he'd already bought the house? The warning bells in her head held a discordant ring. In her logical mind she knew nothing would happen to her that she did not want. Unfortunately, her problem was she did want. She wanted so badly her desire for the viscount kept her up at night and had her touching herself under the covers in ways that the mere thought brought a rush of heat to her face. Mr. Richard Smith's virginal daughter pleasuring herself. The notion was absurd!

"Perhaps, we should come back during the daylight and that way I can see it properly."

"Come let us look at the rooms upstairs," he said as if she hadn't spoken. Placing his hand on the small of her back, he urged her toward the staircase.

Elizabeth looked up at him, her protest poised on the tip of her tongue when she saw the lust in his eyes. But that wasn't what gave her pause; it was the glimmer of satisfaction in making her wary and nervous.

By God, he *knew* she wasn't about to just let him have his way with her. Certainly not before they married. So what was his game?

"And is that where you hope to seduce me?" Her parents would be appalled had they heard her. She was astonished anything in that vein was able to pass her lips.

Lord Creswell didn't respond until they reached the first door on the third floor.

No doubt a bed was on the other side of that door.

He turned to her. "If I may be frank, Miss Smith...Elizabeth." He spoke soft and low, and somehow her name on his lips sounded more intimate than a kiss. "I am a man who likes to leave nothing to chance. If I am to court and marry you in such unfashionable haste, I would like some assurance that you and I suit when it comes to the intimacies of the marriage bed."

At his words, lust in its most pure form accosted her. Parts of her went soft while other parts became rigid, pinpoints of pleasure to come.

No. No. No. There would be no pleasure of any sort. Not for her and definitely none for the viscount.

"So you would like us to have marital relations outside the sanctity of marriage?" she asked in a voice she barely recognized.

"You've been so skittish of late. If I hadn't already kissed you, I'd think you didn't like to be touched. When I marry, it'll be for life and I have no desire to saddle myself with a wife who cannot perform satisfactory in that area." Lord Creswell turned, his back to her as he faced the chamber door. But on his face, she glimpsed the barest hint of smile.

So that was how he thought to get around marrying her. He thought she'd cry off, refusing to enter his philistine game of sampling the goods.

For several long seconds, Elizabeth said nothing, allowing him to believe she was grappling in indecision. His hand released its grasp on the handle of the door and he straightened as if ready to claim victory.

"Very well, if that's what it will take to ease your mind—ease both our minds—let us proceed. But I must have your assurance that once we've established that we suit, um, in that way, we will immediately announce our betrothal and set a wedding date."

Elizabeth took great satisfaction in watching Lord Creswell's entire form stiffen and his hand still in mid-air. Slowly, he angled his head over his shoulder to regard her, incredulity flashing briefly in the blue-green depths of his eyes. "You are in agreement?"

Feigning the stalwartness of that of a virgin about to be sacrificed for the good of God and country, Elizabeth gave a tremulous but firm nod.

"And if we do not suit, what then?"

Did his voice sound a mite strained?

"I have a feeling we shall suit very well." She gave him a slow smile. "Shall we proceed, my lord?"

CHAPTER EIGHT

For an instant, he looked panicked; an expression that probably did not sit comfortably on his face. He then drew a breath, turned and pushed open the door. Elizabeth followed, certain that in any moment, he would surrender as gracefully as a gentleman defeated should.

Given the supposed lack of servants, a lamp on the bedside table was surprisingly lit, lighting the luxuriously furnished room. It contained a large four-poster bed, a wardrobe, a marble-topped vanity and a chest of drawers and smelled freshly cleaned.

Elizabeth proceeded him into the bedchamber remained by the door observing her, studying her with the quiet concentration of a chess player evaluating the board and determining his next move.

He didn't think she would go through with it. Elizabeth could tell that by the faintly cunning look in his eyes.

And perhaps she would not had she known in that very moment, he wouldn't allow it to go that far.

The viscount didn't intend to make love to her, of this she was certain. They were locked in a game of who would blink first.

Abruptly, he closed the door and Elizabeth turned

toward the bed, unwilling to watch his approach, terrified she'd lose her nerve. But she could sense when he stood behind her, still for a moment as if just breathing her in. He smelled of musk and soap and him.

She started when his hands came up and his fingers brushed her nape. It took her a moment to realize he was removing her necklace. His touch was warm and light and her senses went wild.

"I want you naked with not a thing between us."

The warmth of his breath feathered her ear. Her nipples peaked as if he'd laid the flat of his tongue on them. Her center grew moist just thinking about him putting his hands on her, parting her, rubbing her.

This had to stop.

"Beautiful." His praise came out on a breath.

"The necklace?" she asked, intending to tease but her voice cracked too much to carry off such levity.

"That too."

If she turned her head, he would kiss her. She could hear it in the cadence of his breathing and the way he now crowded her, so close his waistcoat brushed intimately against her satin clad back. And how she wanted him to kiss her. But of course she could not. She couldn't allow this to go further.

"Turn around."

Elizabeth gave an involuntary shiver. It wasn't a request. It was a graveled order, velvet over melted steel.

Like a marionette controlled by the master manipulator, she turned slowly unable to stop herself.

She'd thought of naught else since they'd last kissed. Anticipation thrummed through her as she waited, forcing her hands to remain at her side. Just one kiss. It wouldn't go beyond a kiss.

Derek lowered his head, his mouth drawing ever closer to hers. "I want you," he said in a voice fashioned to make a woman instantly wet between her thighs. He fitted his mouth to hers.

Elizabeth automatically reached for the muscled hardness of his shoulders. The feel of him, the taste of his lips sent her already racing heart into a frantic gallop. Her lips opened wider to permit and welcome his searching tongue.

The touch of his tongue against hers had her moaning. He emitted a sound between a laugh and a groan, then his hands were around her, cupping her bottom and pulling her solidly against him. She gasped at the feel of his erection at her center. She could feel him hard and thick through the layers of satin and Indian muslin.

The wanton in her welcomed the undulation of his hips as he ground against her. He did it ever so slowly, like a man who knew how to draw out the pleasure for his mate and extract just as much in return. Elizabeth widened her stance, twining her arms around his neck, as she tried to get closer.

"Damn, I knew it would be this good, feel this good," he muttered darkly, almost as if he resented the fact.

Elizabeth didn't want him to talk. If he was speaking, that meant he wasn't kissing her, and that she could not bear. And one kiss was all they could have.

She brought his lips back to hers with a hard tug and nipped his bottom lip with her teeth, then went about soothing it with her tongue before drawing it into her mouth.

She sucked. He had taught her this, that not only were such intimacies possible but so pleasurable. A harsh groan seemed to originate from the depths of his soul. It spoke of sweet agony and pleasure so acute, it couldn't be tempered or contained.

Time no longer held relevancy. They could have been kissing for seconds, minutes or hours, Elizabeth couldn't be sure. She only knew she never wanted to stop, and she wanted his hands on her breasts—her bare breasts. The ruched peaks of her nipples threatened to bore holes through three layers of fabric.

As if sensing her need, or perhaps acceding to his own, he began removing her gown, releasing the buttons securing it in the back with deft flicks of his fingers, while his mouth continued to devour hers.

Elizabeth permitted it, welcomed the unveiling with an unabashed eagerness that should have made her heat with embarrassment. But as he pushed the blue bodice to her waist, then proceeded to loosen her stays, the slight chill wafting her bared flesh did nothing to cool the fire of his touch. Only when he had her upper body exposed did he lift his mouth from hers, his hooded gaze focused on her breasts with undisguised lust.

"Beautiful," he murmured, his voice throaty and raw.

As if touched by the potency of his regard, her nipples tightened up further into two pointy rose pebbles of need. She wanted his hands on her, his mouth on her. And she thought she'd have her wish in the matter of seconds. But when his hand came up, it wasn't to cup the weight of her breasts, but to take her hand in his. He walked backwards until the lean muscled back of his thighs hit the mattress. His eyes glowed with sensual intent as the candlelight by the bedside caught his handsome features in a luminous, liquid light.

"Remove your dress."

It was the most darkly seductive order she'd ever received. She knew she should put a stop to this before they reached a point of no return. But the demands of her body overrode reason and she began pushing the dress from about her waist.

Derek perched himself on the bed and watched her, his throat working convulsively when he swallowed, the vein at his temple pulsing in tandem with each exhalation of breath.

Her dress landed in a rustle at her feet, soon followed by her lace-edged chemise. She didn't allow herself to think, because in a situation such as this thoughts could be dangerous and chart the error of her ways. But in that moment, she didn't want to be right or proper or strong in her will, she wanted to give into her body's demands.

However, when she was down to only her thin undergarments, she shot a nervous glance at him. His nostrils flared and his pupils dilated. He looked like a man mesmerized, so completely entranced, he'd slipped into another realm of reality.

"The rest." His voice scraped the floor of his throat. "Remove the rest."

Derek pushed aside the warring factions within him—his brain and his cock—forcing himself not to go to her and strip her himself. That wouldn't do at all for he needed to remain in control.

Somewhere between arriving at the house and standing in front of the bedchamber door, his conscience could no longer be smothered or shushed. And Derek found he couldn't so callously seduce her and take her virginity. So instead, he'd challenged her, taunted her, certain her offended very proper virginal sensibilities would send her running pell-mell from the place.

But she hadn't. Which had surprised him. And then he'd been painfully aroused.

Her hands hesitated on the band of her drawers, her nervousness betrayed by a discernible tremble. She inhaled and his gaze was instantly riveted to the thrust of her breasts, firm, full and rose tipped. His breath suspended and his cock felt as if it would explode.

Then she was pushing the offending garment to the floor. Derek took in the cluster of brown curls at the notch of her thighs and wanted to groan at the unfairness of it. A haze of lust blinded him to everything else but her.

"Come." This time he could do no more than grunt.

She came to him all sultry innocence with her gently

rolling hips, on long slim legs and he wanted nothing more than to spread her on the bed, free himself from the constraint of his trousers and sink himself as far into her as he could go. But he could not. He would not take her virginity. He would not risk getting her with child. But by God, he'd take some pleasure with her. That much he'd allow himself. That much he was owed.

"Lean forward." Another dark throaty command.

She did as she was told, stepping between his splayed legs and bracing her hands on his shoulders. Her breasts were where they should be, level with his mouth. Derek flicked the red nub with his tongue. Her skin held the subtle fragrance of some wildflower and tasted...indescribably good. A taste that could easily become addictive.

Her nails dug through the wool of his overcoat into his upper back. That was soon followed by a ragged whimper. He treated her ruched nipple to another swipe of his tongue. Her legs gave away and she sagged into him.

Circling his arms about her waist, he dragged her still closer, keeping her upright as his hands cupped the rounded cheeks of her bottom. He squeezed and kneaded, savoring the feel of delectable, pale, female flesh, so firm and soft.

"Oh," she said on a choked gasp of wonder.

He liked the sounds she made. God, he could not remember wanting a woman more.

Derek didn't know precisely when it occurred. When need obliterated all judicious thought. Gone were the many reasons he could not—should not—take what they both wanted. Lust replaced logic, belated honor lost its valiant fight.

He broke away long enough to divest himself of his clothes. He yanked off his coat, waistcoat and shirt in a frenzy of movement. Frantic fingers made quick work of his trouser buttons. And then finally, thankfully, he was dragging the trousers down over his hips, freeing his erection. Forest green wool crumpled at his ankles and he hastily kicked it off.

The savage in him wanted to part her thighs and sink endlessly into her. But in some lucid functioning part of his brain, he remembered she was a virgin. He had to take it slow.

He groaned into the lower curve of her breast when his cock brushed the sheltering hair between her thighs. He could almost feel her tightness wrapped around him, taking him deep, squeezing him.

Her pants came more rapidly now. She inched her legs apart and he gently pressed them wider as his lips coasted down from the tip of her breast over the peach warmed skin of her belly. Her breath stuttered when his lips reached the tender skin above her sex. With his shoulders, he forced her open to him.

"No, you mustn't." She was staring at him, her expression stricken with embarrassment. "I'm wet." The two words were pained, barely audible. It must have cost her the Earth to utter them.

"That's alright," he soothed, parting her soft, pink

flesh with his fingers. "So is my tongue."

And with that he licked her.

She emitted a high keening sound. Bewildered. Aroused. Her hips jerked, her back coming clear off the bed. Derek stayed with her, steadying her hips in his hand as he licked, tongued and sucked her until she was babbling incoherently, her head thrashing against the pillow. Hips, slim and giving, demanded, cajoled, pled for satisfaction, wider, granting him full access to her swollen, wet heat. He tortured her with long languid strokes before catching the sensitive nub at the hood of her sex between his lips. He worried it with his tongue and then enclosed it in his mouth. He suckled her once, sending her into a paroxysm of pleasure. Her cry, high and plaintive, sounded as if it had been ripped from her throat. Her back bowed tight before she let out a shuddering breath. Then she went limp beneath him, satiated and spent.

God she was glorious. Derek wanted to watch her come again. He wanted to be inside her when she did.

He placed on last kiss on her damp center. She whimpered and her hips undulated in response as she plowed her fingers through his hair. He forced himself to go slow, kissing his way back up her body to swell of her breasts before taking the nipple between his teeth.

"Oh God, Derek."

The thrust of her hips grew in urgency, her nails scoring his scalp, his neck and then sinking into his back. In minutes, she was ready again.

He released her nipple and positioned himself between her thighs, his cock so hard it hurt. He dragged it over her wet folds and her eyes fluttered open. What he saw in them froze him in place.

Bloody hell, he didn't want her affection. It was bad enough he didn't even know what he felt for her anymore. And if he took her virginity…

Derek started to pull away but her legs locked around his waist and her arms manacled his neck.

He groaned. "I can't," he ground the words through clenched teeth as he held himself still against squirming, soft female flesh when all he wanted to do was slide into her.

"I need you," she whispered, panting, her mouth next to his ear. Then she ducked her head and began kissing the side of his neck and bucking her hips until she had his cock prisoned between her legs, snug up against her mound.

Derek's arms trembled but not from physical strain, propped above her as he was trying to play the saint when there wasn't a saintly bone in his body when it came to her.

"Take me." She followed her whimpered command by nipping him on the neck and sliding her hands down his back to grab hold of his buttocks.

Derek couldn't take a second more of her torture. In a flash, he had her arms pinned above her head. If he let her touch him right now, it would be over much too soon.

But she didn't need her hands to excite him and when

she arched against him, demanding her bliss, he thrust hard into her and was encased in her slick heat.

"Sweet Lord, Elizabeth." She was tight. He gritted his teeth as he strived for control. His exit was excruciating slow for he wanted to savor the feel of her, memorize the way her muscles contracted around him. His reentry was swift and jolting.

She gasped, her eyes again closed, her face a picture in ecstasy and her hair a silken tangle on white bed sheets.

Derek experienced pleasure beyond belief. And all too soon his mind released its control to his hips as he pounded into her.

The moment he registered the tremors of her release— the sweet pulsing around his cock—he came utterly and completely undone, giving himself up to an orgasm that wracked his body inside out, wringing him dry. His usual finesse had long abandoned him, and he came down hard on her, drained as he'd never been.

He'd been having sex since the age of fourteen. Sex touched every one of his senses and he knew the feelings each elicited intimately.

Swiftly, he rolled from atop her.

This had not been sex.

It took several minutes to recover, for her body to become her own again, moving under her directive and not his.

Collapsed beside her liked a man who'd been felled by a much greater force, Derek's chest continued to heave, his breaths frequent and ragged.

Outside, the sun had set leaving the room faintly lit by candlelight. Cooling air prickled her sweat-dampened skin. She shivered and reached for the dark green counterpane, a poor substitute for what she really wanted.

In the aftermath of his climax, he'd all but thrown himself from her, their only contact was where the hair on his thigh brushed the baby fine hair on hers. Why hadn't he drawn her into his arms? Was this not the time to pepper her face with tender kisses?

He turned to look at her and nothing in his expression spoke of a man who'd just taken her as if the pleasure of it had to see him through the next ten years. He quickly returned his gaze to the ceiling, one hand propped behind his head.

"Elizabeth Ann Smith, you grew up in Penkridge, Staffordshire in a small cottage with a small parlor and no servants. You have an older sister named Madeline who became acquainted with my younger brother, Henry. She came close to ruining his life," he said in a very flat voice.

Shock rendered her mute and deathly still. Her heart, not yet returned to its normal rhythm, began an erratic thumping in her chest.

Instinctively, her trembling hands yanked the counterpane up to cover her breasts. She bolted to a sitting position.

He allowed his words to permeate before angling a glance in her direction, his eyes cold and remote. "Tell me, Elizabeth, do I have my facts correct?"

Oh God, he knew, was her first painful thought.

But yet he'd made love to her.

How long had he known? came a more disquieting question.

And then *she* knew.

"How long have you known? From the beginning?" Elizabeth desperately needed the answer, yet didn't really want to know.

"Long enough." His tone was brisk and no nonsense.

She clutched the sheet closer to her, now too aware of her nakedness. "So all this time you were—"

"Don't you dare try and turn this on me," he warned between clenched teeth, rising swiftly from the bed. "I was not the one pretending to be someone I'm not."

He located his discarded clothes and began yanking them on. His movements were hurried and abrupt as if he couldn't wait to remove himself from her presence.

"I never once pretended with you. I didn't tell you because I was afraid. I knew you'd think—"

"That you are as much a liar and a conniver as your sister."

Elizabeth's head jerked back, his words as hurtful as a physical blow. Tears pricked the corners of her eyes. "Just as you accepted your brother's word as truth because he is your blood, I feel the same about my sister. I won't sit here while you malign her character."

"I notice you didn't deny that *you* are a liar and a conniver."

"I'm not," she whispered in a choked voice. She was

89

living her worst nightmare, the one day she'd feared the most. "And what of you? Yes, you're correct, I didn't tell you who I was because I knew how you feel about my family. But that is the full extent of my sins. I didn't set to hurt you but you deliberately set out not merely to hurt me, but to ruin me."

Something flickered in his eyes. If he possessed a conscience under all his condescension and judgment, she might have thought it had just been pricked.

"I am no longer a virgin." But in truth, she'd lost more than her virginity the past hour.

He gave a dark laugh and sent her a sidelong glance as he tugged on his trousers. "I did not take your virginity."

Elizabeth blinked certain she hadn't heard him correctly.

"But you did." It wasn't so much as statement as it was a protest.

In a sweeping motion, he gestured toward the bed sheets. "Where is the blood? In any case, I tried to stop but you wouldn't let me go. Did you forget how you were, scratching, biting to get your way," he cruelly reminded her. "I'm no bloody saint. When a beautiful woman begs me to make love to her, who am I to refuse her."

Elizabeth's face burned as she vacillated between shock and shame. In the end, she'd been the sexual aggressor, lustful, demanding and greedy. But despite her behavior and the sexual fire he'd been responsible in igniting in her, she *had* been a virgin.

"Exactly how many virgins have you had?"

He stilled in tucking his shirt into his trousers. His face was in profile so she couldn't see his eyes to try to read him.

After a moment's silence, he resumed dressing. When his clothes were in order, he turned and faced her. "You've played me for a fool once. I'll not let it happen again." His tone held a bitter, hard edge. "I will leave you to dress and await you downstairs."

The door clicked closed seconds later and she was alone. But for the unfamiliar ache between her thighs, she *felt* alone and numb.

The tears fell then. They fell slowly at first before becoming a constant stream, vivid reminders of the crippling pain of heartbreak.

He had deceived her, exacting his vengeance by targeting her where she was weakest. Her desire for him. But she could blame no one but herself for what had taken place tonight. It had been a risky and dangerous game of who would blink first. She'd done a great deal more than blink and for that he would make sure she paid.

Dear Lord, what was she going to do?

She heard his footsteps downstairs where he was undoubtedly impatiently pacing the hall.

Elizabeth scrambled off the bed. At present, she hadn't the time to indulge in self-pity and a good bout of weeping.

As she dressed, she tried not to think about what had occurred on the bed. But for all her attempts to keep the memories at bay, they flooded her thoughts vivid and hot.

She had thought the first time would be painful. That had not been the case. His initial possession had caused a tinge of discomfort, but that had been swept away under a storm of pleasure. So much pleasure.

No, don't think of it.

In order to slip her dress over her head, she had to leave half the buttons unfastened. She pulled on her pelisse and buttoned it up to her neck to hide the way the bodice sagged in the front. She then bundled her mussed hair under her bonnet.

There, she was finished but not ready to face him. Summoning up her courage, she exited the room and descended the stairs.

Derek stood rigid as a palace guard by the front door. His expression was closed and his eyes cold. They proceeded to the carriage parked in front of the residence and completed the journey back to Laurel House in silence.

Upon their arrival at the manor, the viscount insisted on escorting her to the door over her vehement protests. One would imagine he'd be happy to see the back of her.

Why must he insist on torturing me more than he's already done?

Just when Elizabeth had thought the day could not possibly get worse, the front door swung open to reveal her mother standing on the other side.

CHAPTER NINE

"Mama!" It wasn't a greeting. Elizabeth had glimpsed her face in the mirror of the vanity in the bedchambers, and her eyes were red-rimmed, her face a mottled mess.

"Lizzie," her mother practically shrieked in delight.

Soon Elizabeth was enfolded in slender arms, breathing in the scent of her mother's favorite perfume. It reminded her of lilies and the tiny garden they'd had at their home in Penkridge.

Considered a beauty in her time, her mother had managed to maintain much of her looks, her complexion smooth, her brown eyes crinkled lightly at the corners and her hair, light brown and subtly streaked with gray.

Elizabeth found herself hugging her mother's slight frame tightly, suddenly homesick and craving the warmth and loving security of family. But she refused to get misty eyed, especially in front of the viscount.

Her mother set her away from her. "Are you surprised?"

"Mama, what are you doing here? What about the house?"

"I didn't receive a letter from you the week past. You know how I worry."

"But I posted it." Her mother would use any excuse to come to London. But their new residence had been in desperate need of renovations. And her mother trusted no one to oversee the effort and that included Elizabeth's father and sister, Rebecca.

"I did receive a letter from Teresa."

Mrs. Abernathy. Elizabeth suppressed a groan. That explained everything.

It was only then that her mother directed her attention to Derek. He hadn't left but stood quietly behind them watching their reunion.

"Who is this, Lizzie?" Her mother's smile welcomed the viscount. It was obvious she didn't recognize him.

An awkward silence followed. Her mother's smile fell as her gaze darted between them. Two lines formed on her brow.

"Mama, this is Lord Derek Creswell."

A sharpened gaze returned to the viscount. Comprehension dawned on her mother's face. She stood back and switched her scrutiny to Elizabeth.

Elizabeth was immediately conscious of her half-buttoned gown under her pelisse and her disheveled hair under her bonnet.

"Then it would appear the viscount and I are acquainted," her mother's voice had iced over.

Derek acknowledged the fact with a terse nod.

"Elizabeth, remove your things and let us all adjourn to the drawing room where we can speak in private. If Lord Creswell has no objections," her mother added.

There was no way she could remove either the bonnet or the pelisse. And she was certain her sharp-eyed mother was aware of it.

"Mrs. Smi—Lady Bartlett, I'd prefer to speak with you in private."

Relief made Elizabeth almost light-headed. Before her mother could form a response, Elizabeth turned and fled up the stairs and straight into the privacy of her bedchamber.

Lady Bartlett was exactly as Derek remembered her. A petite thing who carried herself with a regal grace that suggested her origins had not been working class or even gentry. Six years ago, he'd thought she'd been simply putting on airs. He wasn't so certain of it now.

Upon entering the drawing room, she dismissed the maid dusting around the fireplace. She settled herself on the sofa and then motioned for him to take a seat.

Derek obliged her, ready for charges that he'd compromised her daughter and demands for a marriage. Six years later, the players were different, but the scenario unchanged.

"Lord Creswell, have you compromised my daughter?" she asked in a most civilized tone.

Derek was taken aback by the question, so very pointed and without the hysterics that had followed the accusation when she'd launched it at his brother. "Is that not a question you should ask your daughter, my lady?"

"I would rather ask you directly. Lizzie has a soft heart

and mightn't tell me the truth."

It would appear the daughters had learned deception at the feet of their mother. She would now act as if they—the whole lot of them—hadn't planned all this down to the smallest detail.

"Your daughter is no worse off than when I first met her."

Her back snapped straighter and her regard narrowed. Anger pursed her mouth. "I want you to stay away from my daughter," she said in excruciatingly crisp tones.

Stay away from my daughter.

It should have brought him relief because it sounded all very good. Seconds elapsed before he concluded the notion settled as well as an overcooked soufflé.

This he hadn't expected. Either the warning or his reaction to it. Indeed, it should be he who should be angry for it was he who had been duped.

"You want me to keep away from her? *Me?*" As if they need worry about him dogging her, unable to stay away for the want of her. Lady Bartlett couldn't possibly mean it. This had to be part of their ploy.

"I certainly am not about to make the same mistake my husband and I made with Maddie when your brother treated her so shamefully."

Derek stiffened in affront. "Your daughter—"

A slender hand shot up to halt his speech. "My daughter," the baroness said, her lips bitterly tight, "was all of seventeen years to your brother's nineteen. Despite claims to the contrary, he was the one who seduced her with promises of a future together and marriage."

"My brother would not lie to me."

"And if you believe that, you're not nearly as bright as you appear."

"I would certainly believe my brother over your daughter."

Lady Bartlett opened her mouth and then abruptly closed it and drew in a breath. "My lord, have you never been wrong about anything or anyone? I shall be the first to admit that I have. I was wrong about you. We met under the most difficult of circumstances and while you struck me as fiercely loyal and protective of your family, you also appeared to be the kind of man who wouldn't make an innocent pay. I know something has occurred between you and my daughter, and I can see she's hurting. But know *this*, Elizabeth is the innocent in all of this. She was fifteen years when this occurred and should not be held accountable."

When the baroness finished, Derek felt all of two feet tall. And he didn't like being brought down so low. Which was probably why, he found himself saying, "Since you have essentially warned me away from your daughter, shall I have a bank dr—"

"I don't want your damn money." She wasn't quite so ladylike now, her eyes flashing in fury, her face shades pinker.

"You demanded it once." That she could not deny.

"It would behoove you to get your facts straight. Neither my husband nor I demanded money. The money was offered."

Derek wasn't accustomed to anyone speaking to him as if he were a child. At least not since he had been one.

The baroness was not yet finished with him. "What would you have done in our place with little money and my daughter's reputation in tatters because of your brother? We lived in a small town, which as you can imagine, made my daughter's marital prospects all but nonexistent. We were forced to settle most of the money on her to ensure a good marriage."

"*My brother* was the injured party. Your daughter knew exactly what she was doing."

They'd been embroiled in the same bitter argument six years ago. Nothing good would come of dredging up the past.

Something fierce flashed in the baroness's eyes. A lioness ready to destroy anything or anyone in order to protect her young. She arose abruptly, her burgundy skirts whirling at her feet. "I will see you out."

Derek didn't know why he was surprised, but he was. No one had ever dismissed him. Ever.

Derek rose. "Elizabeth—"

"Do *not* concern yourself with my daughter," she snapped.

It was clear she suspected he *had* compromised her daughter and she was…letting him go. No demands for marriage and she'd even turned down his offer of money before he'd even managed to make it.

As if she read the confusion in his face, she relented. "I

saw my daughter unhappily married to a man she did not love and did not love her. I won't visit the same misery upon another. I want my girls to be loved and cherished, no matter the cost. If doing so requires that we never again step foot in London, so be it."

Derek digested the news but that was not to say it went down easy. He followed the baroness from the room. He'd never thought about what had happened to Madeline Smith, his anger toward her had been too blind for that.

They arrived in the foyer. A footman stood posted at the front door, which surprised him as Derek hadn't noticed him when they'd arrived.

He turned to the baroness. "Lady Bartlett—"

"Good evening, Lord Creswell," she said with withering finality. She spun on her heel, crossed the foyer and ascended the stairs.

Just as he'd once thought to wash his hands of the whole Smith family, the baroness had obviously washed her hands of him.

This should have relieved him.

It did not.

A knock sounded on Elizabeth's bedroom door ten minutes later.

It was her mother. She had a distinctive *rat-a-tat-tat* knock.

When her mother stepped into the room, Elizabeth

99

knew she knew. But during the next hour in which they spoke, her mother never asked her directly, *Are you still a virgin?* It was as if she didn't want to know. She also said nothing about the conversation she'd had with the viscount and Elizabeth didn't ask. Instead, she shared everything she believed her mother should know: the incident in the garden and Lady Danvers.

Her mother didn't scold her or promise to make things alright, she just opened her arms to her, held her close and whispered, *"If you do nothing else in this life, my dear, marry for love and you'll have no regrets."*

She then asked Elizabeth if she wished to go home with her when she left. But Elizabeth couldn't bring herself to abandon what would undoubtedly be her first and last London Season. And it wasn't because she so adored the social whirl—although it was exciting. No, as much as it pained her to admit it even to herself, especially given his treachery, when she departed London, she would never see him again.

She hadn't given herself to him lightly and couldn't cut him from her heart because she didn't want to feel for him everything she did.

To Elizabeth's surprise, her mother agreed that she should remain in London, reminding her gently to always remember to walk with her head up high.

~*~*~

Two days later, Derek awoke to a misty gray morning

as much a part of London as Newgate and royalty. By the time he arrived at White's for a prearranged meeting with Cartwright, his mood was black as the night skies.

They took a table on the second floor and spoke of the mundane as they played *all fours* before Derek collected the cards at the close of the second game and carefully placed the deck on the redwood surface between them.

With a pointed look at the cards and then at Derek, Cartwright raised a quizzical brow. "Is it the prospect of your upcoming nuptials that has you looking so morose or can that be blamed on the company?" his friend asked wryly.

"I will not be wedding Miss Smith."

Cartwright's mouth flattened into a straight line. "Pardon?" he asked in a deceptively soft voice. The calm before the storm.

"Before you call me out, at least do me the courtesy of listening to what I have to say." They lived in modern times but duels were not beyond the realm of possibility, although he imagined it'd be Rutherford he'd be meeting across the field at dawn. Derek hoped it wouldn't come to that.

Cartwright's jaw was tight as if he were gritting his teeth. He jerked his chin motioning Derek to continue.

And so he recounted the tumultuous history between the families—an incident he hadn't shared with a soul—and his meeting with the baroness.

At the conclusion, his friend let out a single expletive. "Doesn't she give a damn that her daughter will be disgraced?"

"Apparently she'd rather that than have me as a son-in-law." Which made not one whit of sense. If Elizabeth married him, she'd want for nothing.

Except a husband who loved her.

Bloody hell, the woman had told him to stay away from her daughter. Why was he still thinking about Elizabeth? When would it stop? Missing her? Wanting her?

"Hell, you called her eldest daughter a liar and a gold digger and insinuated she and her husband were extortionists. Did you expect her to smile prettily and welcome you with open arms?" Cartwright asked, his voice low and fierce, his form nearly vibrating like a plucked tine.

Derek's back stiffened in affront. "I merely spoke the truth. Good God man, I was there."

"No, your brother was there not you. You have only his word he didn't seduce the girl and divest her of her virginity."

"His word is good enough for me."

Cartwright had the gall to look skeptical.

"And Miss Smith, the one you *did* compromise, what do you intend to do about her? She's in need of a husband."

Not one hour passed when he didn't think about her, when he didn't remember what she'd looked like naked on the bed, the glossy sheen of her tangled hair spread against the stark whiteness of the bed sheets. He remembered too her quiet smile, her soft laugh, her inquisitive eyes and easy company.

If she had been anyone else than *who* she was, he would have married her.

But all the *ifs* in the world wouldn't change that he couldn't trust her.

"She doesn't need a husband," Derek replied quietly, thinking about the report on his desk. "I've taken care of that."

Derek saw his brother once a year, which was not at the height of the London Season. Henry normally packed up his brood at Christmastide to make the trip to the estate in Berkshire, the location of the viscountcy seat. But when Derek returned to his residence the day after he'd spoken with Cartwright, he found his brother reclining in his favorite chair in the library.

"What the devil are you doing here?" As much as he loved his younger brother, Derek wasn't exactly fit for company. He and Cartwright hadn't parted on cordial terms or spoken since.

And it had been three days since he'd last seen Elizabeth. He hated that that even signified.

His brother pushed his lanky frame from the chair, the same easy grin he'd used to charm his way out of plenty of trouble beamed from his face.

"Hey old man, you're looking quite prosperous." He

thrust out his hand, which Derek shook as he tamped down a niggling sense of irritation. This old business with Henry was now more than a thorn in his side, it now haunted him.

"As are you. What have I done to deserve a visit?" Derek motioned his brother back into his chair, while he took the one opposite.

"Well, if you want to know the truth, I heard the most ghastly rumor and thought I'd come up and get the truth right from the horse's mouth—so to speak."

Elizabeth. There could be no other reason.

When Derek didn't immediately respond, Henry tilted his head to the side, his dark brow propped high. "Would you like to know what I heard?"

"I'm sure you didn't come all this way to not tell me."

His brother abandoned his indolent pose and came forward in his seat. "I can see that it's true. You are courting the younger Smith girl." Henry made it an accusation.

Derek didn't very much care for his tone.

"And if I am?" Derek wasn't certain he hadn't said it just to be contrary.

His brother went silent as if his power of speech had suddenly abandoned him. Unfortunately, he found it soon enough.

"Have you gone completely mad, man? After our dealings with that family?" Henry asked, the whites of his eyes clearly visible.

"This matter is none of your concern." The very, very

last thing Derek wished to discuss with his brother was Elizabeth Smith.

Henry's eyes narrowed. He then asked softly as if his suspicion had not yet been fully realized, "Did you bed her?"

Derek came abruptly to his feet. This discussion was officially over. "I just told you that my relationship with Miss Smith is my personal affair and therefore, no concern to you."

Relationship. Derek wasn't sure who was more stunned by his injudicious use of the word, him or his brother. And this after having had her once and knowing her the duration of three weeks.

"Did she tell you that you were her first? I hope you didn't believe her. Her sister said the same to me."

It took a moment before Derek understood the full import of his brother's vehement claim. His mind reeled and his belly lurched sickly. If betrayal had a sound, at present it was buzzing in his ears. When he finally spoke, his voice was low and too controlled. "You told me you hadn't bedded her. You swore it on our grandmother's grave."

A look of sheepishness flashed across his brother's face. It lasted but a moment. "What else did you expect me to say? I certainly wasn't going to marry her." His mouth curled in disdain. "I knew if I told you the truth, you would puff up your chest and lecture me on honor, integrity and that sort of thing."

Derek clenched his hands into fists, forcibly holding

them pinned to his sides lest he strike his brother as he greatly yearned to. Instead he breathed, drawing in large drafts of air into his lungs. "I went to their home, stood in the middle of their parlor and called their daughter a gold-digger—insinuated she was little more than a whore."

"She was a gold-digger. The fact that I shagged her in no way changes that. I probably wasn't the first man she'd tried it with. You thought as much yourself."

Blood rushed to Derek's head as blinding rage threatened to obliterate his vision. "I believed so based on your word. You swore it had been a kiss and nothing more." He spat the last two words.

"Good God man, that was six years ago. Why the hell are you getting all heated up over it now?"

Derek stared into his brother's brown eyes and saw with amazing clarity the type of man he'd become—perhaps had always been—but he, his older brother, had been too blind to see. Selfish and spoiled, a man who lacked the proper moral compass. If he wasn't his flesh and blood, Derek would have pummeled him to a fare thee well.

"Your behavior was then, and is now, unconscionable." As admonishments went, Derek's lacked the frenzied rage one might expect given the seething anger inside him.

His brother stared at him for several moments, clearly puzzled by his reaction. Then his brows smoothed and the semblance of smile angled the corners of his mouth upward. "You care for her," he whispered as if voicing an astounding revelation.

Denial sprang immediately to his lips. Derek opened his mouth to issue it with emphatic conviction when an image of Elizabeth, naked with rose-tipped breasts and passion glazed eyes, pushed unwanted into his thoughts.

The silence that followed was its own response.

Henry shook his head, his expression bemused. "By God, I was right. You've gone and fallen for the chit."

It happened before Derek could stop himself. His fist met his brother's jaw with a thud. There was a roar of pain and then Henry staggered back several steps, his hand cradling the left side of his face that in minutes would begin to swell and distort as bone crunching blows tended to do.

"Bloody hell, Derek, what the devil!"

His brother look bewildered as if all he'd done shouldn't have given Derek cause to lay him low even before he had the temerity to speak of Elizabeth in such disparaging tones. To speak about her as if she was some insignificant piece of baggage who didn't deserve respect.

"You had that coming. Consider yourself lucky that you're my brother or I would've broken your damn jaw." And he could have hit him a great deal harder.

"Make certain you're not here when I return." With that and sore reddened knuckles, Derek stalked from the room.

CHAPTER TEN

Elizabeth's mother stayed, taking up the role of her chaperone until the family returned from Devon where Lady Armstrong had given birth to a baby girl.

They attended two balls, one excessively stuffy supper party and saw a comedy at Drury Lane. Derek had been notably absent from all.

Elizabeth didn't see him *anywhere*.

He hadn't been with Lord Alex when he'd come to visit James. And from the idle talk she'd heard at the balls, it appeared he'd suddenly and completely dropped out of society.

Elizabeth tried very hard not to think on it too much. Unfortunately, *trying* did not guarantee success. Her heart literally ached and an indescribable feeling of loss swamped her.

Her cousin's twins, two-year-old Jason and Jessica took to her mother immediately. And who wouldn't? She spoiled them terribly buying them toys and sneaking them treats from the dessert cart after they'd already been put to bed.

On the fifth day of her visit, her mother announced she'd be returning home the following day. She claimed she must to ensure her husband—who had trouble discerning green from blue—didn't instruct Mr. Birch, the house decorator, to paint the guest chamber a perfectly objectionable color.

With a promise to return to escort Elizabeth home, which was little over a week away, she was off and everyone was genuinely sad to see her go.

The evening following her mother's departure, Elizabeth went to Lady Templeton's ball with Charlotte, Catherine, Missy and James, determined to enjoy herself. It was looking more likely than naught, that this ball would be the last of the few to which she would be invited.

They were there a full half-hour when Derek strode through the towering ornate doors of the ballroom.

Elizabeth inhaled sharply and released it on a prolonged sigh. Relief, anxiety, anticipation and heartbreak mingled in one breath.

She ate him up with her eyes; with the sort of gluttony that brought her both pain and pleasure. She watched the way his loose limbed strides covered the floor. She devoured his fine form. Things she ought not to be doing if she possessed any sort of restraint or self-preservation.

He stopped to greet their hostess, and something in that greeting gave the impression of warm familiarity. It was in the way Lady Templeton touched his arm and his amused laugh when the marchioness whispered something in his ear.

Lady Templeton was incredibly lovely, blond and

quite buxom, but she was old enough to be his mother. And she was married.

Jealousy pecked with woodpecker glee at her insides. Elizabeth quickly averted her gaze from the sight of the two together, forcing herself to concentrate on Catherine, who currently carried on a conversation with Miss Dawn Hawkins.

But try as she might, Elizabeth found it impossible to follow their conversation. Her thoughts and gaze kept drifting to a Lord Creswell, who was devastatingly handsome clad in his white cravat and black tails.

He turned, his gaze searching the room until he found her, and there it settled. He said something to the countess and started toward Elizabeth, his long purposeful strides closing the distance between them rapidly. All this he did without once removing his gaze from her.

Elizabeth's heart felt as if it had scrambled into her throat. Breathing became a ridiculous chore requiring too much thought and coordination. As he drew closer, she didn't blink fearing she'd discover this was naught but a dream.

When he was finally standing in front of her, he bowed a formal, elegant bow and spoke her name, which came out more a verbal caress.

"Good evening, ladies." He dipped his head in a bow toward Catherine and Miss Hawkins. Catherine responded with a shallow curtsy and Dawn Hawkins preened.

"Miss Smith, may I have the next dance?"

He was requesting a dance. Or was this another game?

Elizabeth shook her head. "My lord—"

"I refuse to take no for an answer." He advanced a step and now stood entirely too close.

Elizabeth tore her gaze from his and darted a glance around. They were being watched with unabashed interest by far too many guests. Catherine nodded, a barely discernible forward tip of her head, silently communicating that a refusal would be most unadvisable.

Not if Elizabeth didn't want to cause a scene. And she refused to enter into another game of who would blink first with the viscount.

Her acceptance came silently, a white, silk gloved hand on his proffered arm. With that contact, instant heat coursed through her, jolting her. She might have pulled off her glove—appropriately white in color—and waved it over her head to signal her surrender had her surrender been wholly complete. This was a dance, nothing more.

Much in the same way Buckingham was merely a house and Victoria a simple woman who happily took up residence there.

The viscount kept his gaze fixed on her as he escorted her to the center of the dance floor where they joined the couples lined up to commence a quadrille.

The music rang out, setting more than three dozen couples into synchronized motion. They moved smoothly and in such harmony one would think they'd danced together for years. But the act of making love, was that not its own lusty, hip pounding, heart thudding dance?

His fingers curled around hers, possessive and firm.

Their eyes met, his smoldering with an intensity that shortened her breaths and set her heart a pounding. She blinked and looked away.

After several minutes, when her curiosity would go unappeased a moment longer, she asked, "What are you doing?"

His mouth quirked to one side. "I am dancing. Is my technique so poor?"

They came apart. He twirled her twice. He circled her wide and then drew her close. His dancing was impeccable, as well he knew.

"Are you forgetting you don't like me? You believe I'm one of those lying conniving Smiths." She forced a smile but spoke with a soft savageness she hoped would wound him the same way he'd wounded her.

"Believe me...I like you more than well enough." He regarded her mouth as his thumb furtively stroked the top of hers.

She felt the intimacy of his touch through her glove. Needles of pleasure spread throughout her like heat on flesh numb from cold. The resurgence of feeling relief, joy and pain.

Before she embarrassed herself by doing something as silly as wilting to the floor, the dying strains of the cello signaled the end of the dance. Saved.

"Shall we?" Derek proffered his right arm. She accepted, momentarily grateful to have something solid to keep her upright.

Her crutch proved to be the very thing she required a

crutch for. But she didn't remove her hand. More of that gluttony she suffered from.

For the area skirting the dance floor, standing room was at a premium. Derek handled the swell of guests with ease, maneuvering them expertly until the press of bodies thinned, where one could breathe.

They passed a surprisingly well-dressed Lady Danvers, who refused to meet her gaze, which was odd as Elizabeth had never seen the dowager looking so ill at ease. Since the evening in the garden, the dowager had cornered her at several events slyly inquiring about the upcoming announcement. The dowager had been like a cat toying with a mouse certain that one of her swipes would draw blood.

Elizabeth wasn't quite certain when she realized Derek was leading her farther and farther away. Where guests no longer surrounded them but were now voices at their backs, and the surroundings weren't so brightly lit. But once she realized, she halted.

She'd once tread this perilous path before. It had landed her behind a hedgerow with a charming lord. The same path had had her giving away her innocence, the consequences, hers and hers alone to bear. This was the path her sister had taken and forever lived to regret. She'd be three times the fool to tread down it again.

CHAPTER ELEVEN

Elizabeth dropped her hand from his arm. "I'm going back to the ball." Her voice wasn't all that strong but her will was.

"Elizabeth… Please." It wasn't his tentative touch on her arm that halted her mid-stride but the entreaty in his voice. She felt scalded by it.

If she had any sense at all, she'd leave. But he'd never spoken to her like that before. As if he'd yearned for her from a distance and now she was within reach. So she stayed because when it came to her dealings with Derek Creswell, rational thinking sprouted wings and flew out the front door, attaining heights far out of mortal reach.

She was just a flesh and blood woman.

She turned and peered up at him. He even *looked* different. The way he looked at her; it was softer, wistful almost. As if she was no longer that Elizabeth Smith of Penkridge, Staffordshire, somehow connected to all that was treacherous and wicked in the world.

"What is it you want from me, Derek?" He'd made it clear he wasn't going to marry her, so perhaps he thought to have her as his mistress.

And foolish *foolish* girl that she was, she didn't know

she would refuse him.

"Not here." He glanced around. "Let us speak in private."

The hallway was dimly lit and empty save them, but the entrance to the great room was within sight. Anyone could venture out and see them.

She hesitated a moment before relenting with a nod.

Taking her hand in his, he led her down a narrow hallway that branched from where they'd been.

"It seems you know this house intimately," she murmured, not exactly accusing him of other intimacies with one of the female occupants she couldn't bear to think of.

"I played here as a child. Lord and Lady Templeton are as close to me as family. I practically grew up with their son," he responded, with a brief look down at her.

With those words, Elizabeth no longer wanted to hang the very lovely Marchioness of Templeton in effigy. His explanation certainly explained the easy familiarity between him and the lady of the manor. "Where are you taking me?"

"Somewhere no one will interrupt us," came his cryptic response.

She nearly pulled back then. Interrupt them from doing what? Did he intend to...do anything untoward? Here of all places? The thought did *not* arouse her or fill her with wicked anticipation.

He must have taken her hesitation as trepidation for he tightened his hold on her hand, angled his head down slightly and whispered in her ear, "Trust me."

Trust him as much as he trusted her? That was reason enough for her to leave that instant. But she didn't. She stayed because, ironically, she did trust him.

Seconds later, he pushed open the door to a room and ushered her inside. A quick glance around revealed a room really the size of a rather large closet furnished with a small writing desk, one solitary bookshelf, a cushioned armchair and a reading gas lamp. The lamp was unlit but light poured in through a passageway from the adjoining room. Elizabeth gathered this was the antechamber to the study or library.

Derek released her hand, removed his gloves and quickly lit the lamp. With deft efficiency, he fished into his jacket pocket and pulled out a key, which he used to open the desk drawer. The contents of the drawer now had Elizabeth's focused attention. She watched as he picked up a sheaf of papers—no more than four in number—and handed them to her.

In dull surprise, she looked down at the papers filled with bold masculine scrawl now clasped in her hand and then back at him. "What is this?" she asked.

His mouth curved and his eyes seemed to light from within. Elizabeth didn't think she'd ever seen anything quite as beautiful as his smile.

"With that report you are ensured Lady Danvers will never breathe a word of what she witnessed that evening in the garden. She will in fact *never* be a threat to your reputation whether you marry or not. I will even go as far to say she could see you prancing about as naked as the day you were born and would never speak a word of it."

The individual words, Elizabeth understood, but together they colluded to confuse her and send her mind into a tailspin. And not because she was daft *but* because the notion didn't seem possible. "What did you—? How could you have—? Do I even want to know?" She stared blindly down at the papers in her hand. Her mind registered dates and Italy and the name Vincent.

He laughed softly and smiled tenderly.

"Let us just say Lady Danvers is anxious that a certain Vincent Trifoli remain in Italy. He has more than a passing resemblance to her son and heir, Steven. They became acquainted forty-five years ago, just ten months shy of the earl's birth."

"The Earl of Danvers?" Elizabeth asked in a hushed voice.

Derek nodded.

And the dowager had had the nerve to lecture *her* on morality? It was beyond the pale, yet somewhat satisfying to know that the dowager couldn't lord the incident over her anymore.

But that meant... She furrowed her brows. Why had he gone to the trouble of digging up the dowager's past?

"But why would you do that? You never intended to marry me. I thought you *wanted* to see me ruined."

He flinched at that. Reaching out his hand, he grasped her wrist and pulled her inexorably closer. In silence, he slowly peeled the glove from her hand and dropped it on the desk beside his. He then did the same to the other.

"I'm sorry. I was wrong," he said, his voice deep and low. He drew her into his arms.

Elizabeth went stiff. He had been wrong about so many things. "Wrong about what precisely?"

"Your sister. I spoke with my brother and he admitted to bedding her," he said grimly.

Madeline. He was sorry about her sister. That had been the one thing she'd understood—his loyalty to his brother. She was happy he'd learned the truth but—

"I have something for you." He released her and moved toward the bookshelf.

Elizabeth immediately missed the warmth of his arms.

From one of the upper shelves, he retrieved a glossy wood figurine measuring approximately a foot and a half in height.

"You once asked to see my work and asked if I ever sculpted people. I told you only if I found them interesting enough. Well no one has interested me more than the subject of this one." He offered the carving to her.

Dazed, Elizabeth accepted it, her fingers registering the smoothness of the shiny surface. It was a woman bedecked in a lovely ball gown, her head angled over her shoulder. The lace on the gown had been intricately carved as were the combs decorating her hair. She was slim and slightly full in the breasts, and the face…the face was undeniably hers. It was beautiful.

Her breath hitched, her hands began a violent trembling and her eyes grew wide as her gaze flew up to his. Tears burned the back of her eyes.

"This is how I first saw you, peeking at me over your shoulder. That image has remained ingrained in my mind since."

"Derek." His name came out choked as emotion seared her throat.

"I don't want you to marry me for fear of ruination. I want you to marry me for the same reason I want to marry you. For love."

Elizabeth didn't have the capacity to speak. At least not with any proficient articulation. She was buffeted by too many emotions, all of them overwhelming. She let out an uneven breath.

"I will be forever grateful that Lady Danvers is the biggest gossip in all of Christendom."

She smiled despite the tears beginning to fall.

"That," he glanced pointedly at the wood carving of her, "is yours only if you agree to marry me. If you refuse me, I will have to keep it as it will be all that I have of you." He wore his vulnerability on his face, his eyes exhibiting a caution she'd never seen before, his voice low and uncertain.

Carefully and with undue care, Derek extricated *his gift* from her trembling hands and placed it on the desk. It was then she noticed the adhesive plaster wrapped around his index finger.

Instantly concerned, she asked, "What happened?" Her voice was barely above a whisper.

He chuckled softly and held up his finger. "It's just a

nick from the carving knife. I gave myself three days to finish and I succeeded with only minor war wounds."

Elizabeth's vision blurred as a sob wracked her frame. He immediately enclosed her in his arm and she buried her face into the crook of his shoulder, melting into the hard contours of his body.

He leaned down and pressed a possessive kiss against her lips. "I was your first—"

A heartfelt apology.

"—and I want to be the only man in your life."

A heartfelt declaration.

"Will you do the honor of agreeing to be my wife?"

A proposal.

She let out a shuddery breath. "Oh," she said in a small voice.

Keeping her in the tight circle of his arms, Derek sank into the chair behind him, tumbling Elizabeth into his lap.

He quirked his brow. "Oh? That is all?"

Elizabeth found it hard to speak, now distracted by his erection pressing up against her bottom. She choked down a sob.

"*Shhh*, my love," he said gently wiping a tear with his thumb.

Elizabeth had never *felt* so much in all her life. Her feelings were just too big, too extraordinary, too exhilarating.

"I love you," she whispered.

Her acceptance.

And then she kissed him.

120

EPILOGUE

Elizabeth came slowly awake to the familiar press of an erection against her bum. She pressed back to gauge the level of his willingness—her husband's readiness was never in question.

A rumbled groan sounded from behind her as strong hands gripped her hips and brought her naked form flush against his equally naked front. His chest hairs gently abraded the soft skin of her back. With his hands still holding her hips in place, he pressed his erection into her, his breath harsh and labored near her ear.

Elizabeth didn't even try to hold back the moan that slipped heedless from her lips—could deny him nothing not even the sound of her pleasure. Moisture collected at her center readying her for his possession. She couldn't remember once in their eight month marriage when she hadn't been.

Months ago, she'd stopped being amazed how she could crave Derek's touch so intensely and want him with such frequency. She just accepted it for what it was as one in the many ways they expressed their desire and love for each other.

"Good morning. Lift your leg," he urged, his voice

passion drugged.

Elizabeth eagerly obliged him, raising her leg inches before Derek took control.

Sometimes he would linger, running his fingers languidly down the length of her thigh before reaching her knee. This morning he was impatient, sinking into her in one smooth thrust, filling her to capacity. Impaled, she could only whimper and moan at the sheer pleasure of his possession.

Need clawed wildly within her. He pulled almost out and then slammed back into her with enough force to make her toes curl and her knees to shake in his hands as he held her open for him. Her breath came in ragged gasps as he pummeled her, in and out, repeating the movements until her vision blurred.

With a sinuous arch of her back, she thrust her bottom back hard on a downward stroke. He hissed out a breath between clenched teeth as if in pain.

From there, things got wild and out of control. They labored like that for several minutes, the race to satisfaction, the promise of nirvana just strokes away.

When her climax hit, it ripped through her with the strength of a tornado, and defying gravity, flung her up to the stars. Only after she found her release, did Derek take his. With one final thrust, he spent himself inside her, her name a violent groan on his lips.

Elizabeth could barely catch her breath. Her skin was damp and rosy from exertion and satiation. She lay in her husband's arms utterly spent.

Slowly he pulled out of her and pushed the length of her tangled hair over her shoulders. A soft kiss landed on her neck. She loved when he did this, loved basking in the afterglow. The scratch of his stubble had her reaching up with her free hand to lovingly rub his cheek.

"Was I too rough?" His lips coasted the shell of her ear.

"Never." It came out sounding like a purr.

"No nausea?"

With a playful nip to her ear, Derek dropped his head onto the pillow. Elizabeth rolled onto her side to face him, propping up on her elbow.

She smiled down at him. "Not this morning."

"Maybe I should always wake you like that." As he spoke, his gaze drifted to her breasts.

She chuckled. "But you do."

He continued to eye her breasts. "Do they still hurt?"

Before she could answer, he lightly brushed her nipple with his thumb until it pebbled. They had discovered she was with child the month before and now in the third month of her pregnancy, she was starting to see a slight rounding to her stomach.

"Not when you do that." Her release only minutes before had rendered her practically enervated but his touch began a slow simmer of pleasure in her blood. But sadly, they didn't have time for another bout of lovemaking.

"Derek, you know we cannot. There isn't time. Charlotte would never forgive me if I came late to her wedding."

"Good God, is that today already?" he teased. Elizabeth had talked of little else the past fortnight.

The marriage was to have taken place six months ago, but the death of Alex's brother and heir to the duchy had made it necessary to move it forward so a year of mourning could be observed.

Lung fever had taken Alex's brother Charles in a matter of weeks. But now things appeared to be better. Alex was slowly healing from the loss with Charlotte's unwavering love and support. If any two people deserved happiness, those two certainly did.

Elizabeth and Derek's own wedding had been held at St. George's and was well attended by *ton's* standards. No blood had been spilled when his brother and her sister saw each other for the first time in over six years. And he and her parents had buried the past upon Derek's apology.

Elizabeth could happily say, it had been one of the most memorable and wonderful days in her life. And in six months, they would welcome the birth of their own child.

"If they are even half as happy as we are, they will be truly blessed." She leaned down and placed a feather of a kiss on his lips, pulling back when he tried to take it deeper, hunger evident in his eyes.

He smiled, chagrined and then oh so tenderly ran the back of his hand down her cheek. "I count my blessings every day."

THE END

SNEAK PEEK

AN HEIR OF DECEPTION

Abandoned at the altar...

A man devastated by love

After three years of carousing and debauchery, Alex Cartwright, heir to the Duke of Hastings, has put his life back in order. Having embraced sobriety for two years, he has no intention of revisiting the past or risking his heart again. But the return of the very woman who introduced him to the darkest side of hell brings not only the painful, haunting memories of bittersweet love and abandonment, but the son he never knew he had...

A woman silenced by secrets

Threatened by the revelation of a secret that could destroy her family's place in society and forever tarnish a dukedom, Charlotte fled England on her wedding day five years ago. Now, although it appears that secret is safe, when Alex discovers her other secret—their son—Charlotte has an altogether different battle ahead. She must now fight one love to hold onto the other—the man whose touch still makes her burn, for the child who is her very world.

London, 1859

A hushed silence greeted Alex Cartwright's arrival into an antechamber in St. Paul's Cathedral.

Attired in navy frock coats, precisely knotted neckties, and light blue trousers, the Viscount Armstrong and Rutherford, the Earl of Windmere, were certainly suited up well enough for the occasion. At least in dress if not demeanor, for their faces held the grayish cast of men bound for the gallows. And Rutherford's hair appeared as if it had been plowed more times than a seasoned whore.

Pausing just inside the threshold, Alex let out a dry laugh. "Come now gentlemen, it can't be as bad as that," he teased. "The occasion does not call for black dress or armbands. This isn't a funeral you're attending, but my wedding."

Such a comment would have customarily elicited a wry smile, at the very least. Neither man blinked and another silence the weight of a ship's anchor descended upon the room, blanketing him in air as cold as London's fog was thick.

Determined that whatever their affliction, it would not spoil the most important day thus far in his twenty-eight years, Alex quelled the sense of unease beginning to unfurl in his gut.

Under a domed celestial frieze of cherubs and angels, Alex advanced toward the pair standing motionless in front of a large marble-topped table, his footfall muffled by the carpeted floor. He would have welcomed more noise, some sort of distraction from the somberness surrounding him, be it in human form or décor.

Located in the south transept of the church, the chamber boasted dark burgundy drapes of some thick, expensive fabric, and surrounding the black marble fireplace were three chairs crafted with enough gild, scrollwork, and velvet to satisfy royalty. But then, with the sudden death of his brother—the much beloved son and heir to the Hastings dukedom—wasn't Alex now regarded as such? Despite his mother's vehement opposition to the marriage, when Alex had made it clear he'd marry Charlotte with or without her approval, she thrown her considerable ducal weight into ensuring his wedding would be the most celebrated event in Society for at least the next decade to come.

Halting in front of his friends, he quirked a brow. "Surely you're not commiserating over my nuptials?" Alex found light sarcasm served as a wonderful vehicle to lift a dour mood. "I would think not, as you both have walked—" He executed a mock bow. "I stand corrected gentlemen—vanquished this course years ago."

2

And most assuredly they had, both men happily married with nary a complaint regarding the oft-bemoaned rigors of the institution. Indeed, each had been passionate in its recommendation.

Armstrong shot Rutherford a look, one Alex instantly recognized. He'd seen it often enough over the course of an acquaintance numbering twenty-six years. In that instant, he knew something was terribly, perhaps tragically, wrong.

Panic bloomed and anxiety burned like acid in his throat. Alex's gaze flew to Rutherford. "It's Charlotte isn't it? Something has happened to Charlotte."

The earl averted his gaze.

In an abrupt move that brought the two men practically nose to nose, Alex grabbed Rutherford forcibly by the arms. Even if his friend's delay had been infinitesimal, it measured what felt like an eternity too long.

Holding the other man in a vise grip, Alex gave him a teeth-jarring shake. "Tell me damn it. What's happened to Charlotte? Is she hurt? Where is she?"

Bending his imprisoned arm at the elbow, Rutherford offered up an envelope. "She sent this for you," he said hoarsely.

Dropping his hands to his sides, Alex took a cautious step back. At first, he could only stare at the innocuous rectangular paper, uncomprehending, a little dazed. Slowly, the fog released its hold on his senses.

His gaze darted to the sheaf of paper crushed in

Rutherford's other hand. He then recalled the footman hurrying down the hall. In that instant, he knew the man he'd passed with so little regard, so consumed with his own happiness, had been the bearer of the news that had sent his friends into this morbid melancholy. News that would assuredly send him someplace far worse.

Charlotte wasn't hurt. The evidence stood before him in the form of her brother. Had she been injured or taken ill, a stable full of horses wouldn't have been able to drag Rutherford from her side. But too swiftly on the heels of staggering relief nipped a growing fear. For penned in her signature slopes and curls was his name emblazoned across the front of the envelope. A letter from her on the day of their wedding could signify only one thing.

"She's not coming is she?" His cravat—silk mulberry that his valet had fussed into an elaborate knot—felt as if it had a stranglehold on his words.

"Cartwright—"

Alex's head jerked violently in the direction of his friend, the set of his countenance effectively cutting Armstrong off at the utterance of his name.

With a hefty sigh, Armstrong ran his hand through his thatch of golden hair, regarding him with eyes filled with the kind of compassion no man should have to countenance on his wedding day. Sympathy was bad enough, but pity, intolerable.

Directing his attention back to Rutherford, Alex stared at the envelope unclaimed in his friend's hand

4

knowing its contents promised to deliver him the felling blow.

"What does she say?" he asked, his voice a hollow imitation of his former self.

"I didn't read it," Rutherford muttered gruffly, extending his arm so the tan paper touched the bare flesh exposed at Alex's wrist.

Alex jerked back at the contact and retreated several steps, surveying it with abhorrence, like something truly reprehensible.

"What did she tell you?" he asked quietly, dragging his gaze up to Rutherford's.

Six months ago when his friend had paced the halls outside his wife's bedchamber awaiting the birth of their third child, he'd worn the same expression he did at present, a helpless sort of fright.

"What does she say!" Alex's voice exploded like a cannon blast in graveyard silence. "Isn't it in the letter she sent to you?"

Isn't it in the letter she sent to you? The echo transcended the room to storm the corridors of the prestigious church.

Rutherford appeared to have to rally his courage, swallowing, and then drawing in a ragged breath before he said, "The footman brought the letters only moments before your arrival. I was coming—"

"God dammit man, quit all your blasted blathering. Just tell me what she wrote!"

Rutherford made an uncomfortable sound in his

throat before replying in graveled tones, "She wrote to beg my forgiveness for any scandal or shame her actions may bring upon the family but…says she can't marry you."

A roar sounded in Alex's ears as he grasped the back of a nearby chair, the coolness of the metal frame muted by his silk white gloves. He blinked rapidly in an effort to halt the stinging in his eyes and swallowed to douse the burning in his throat. And a numbness such as he'd never known assailed him turning his limbs into leaden weights.

"Where is she?"

Stark pain and fear flashed in Rutherford's pale blue eyes. "I don't know. She's quit the Manor but gave no indication as to where she's gone. She merely states she is safe and that we must not concern ourselves unduly over her."

The weight on Alex's chest threatened to crush every organ beneath it. But such destruction would do little to his heart, for it had already broken into a multitude of pieces.

Like that, with the flourish of a pen, she was gone.

Turning, Alex made for the open door. Around him, he felt rather than saw his friends move in chorus toward him. He stopped abruptly, angled his head over his shoulder and met their gazes. "Let me be. I shall be fine." But he wouldn't lie to himself; he would never be fine.

The two men did not advance any further.

Alex blindly put one foot in front of the other. With every step, he discarded a piece of the dream of the life he'd foolishly thought to have with her...until there were none.

He took his leave of the room, his leave of the church, to start his way back to a life obliterated to a pile of nothingness.

CHAPTER ONE

Berkshire, 1864

Her sister was gravely ill.

The knowledge plagued Charlotte Rutherford, consuming her with such fear that a proper night's sleep had been impossible since her good friend, Lucas Beaumont had informed her upon his return from England.

The news had catapulted her into a frenzy of activity for two days thereafter. In that time, she'd arranged passage to England and closed up her small townhouse in Manhattan. What came next required all of her endurance: an eleven-day voyage across the Atlantic Ocean. With too much time to her solitary thoughts, she'd been wracked with inconsolable grief and the bitterest regret...and heart stopping fear that her presence there would open a Pandora's Box of a different sort.

Now two weeks to the day after she had learned of her sister's illness, Charlotte was here. The place she'd once called home. And after an absence of nearly five years, the reality of once again being on English soil—

standing at the doors of Rutherford Manor—brought with it the heartbreak of old.

All of that, however, paled in the light of her sister's illness. For Katie, Charlotte would endure anything, even if it meant risking exposure and opening a wound that had never healed. One she feared might never *truly* heal.

With her heart in her throat and anxiety now a familiar—albeit unwelcome—companion, Charlotte lifted the knocker of the oak door and brought it down three times in rapid succession.

The ensuing seconds seemed to stretch on endlessly. Were they home? She hadn't even considered that possibility when she'd arrived in Town and had proceeded directly to Paddington Station to catch the train to Reading. She shot a glance over her shoulder and regarded the phaeton parked in front of her hired coach. Someone must be in residence, as it appeared they had company. Something else she hadn't considered.

At the opening of the door, she gave a nervous start and spun back around. Reeves, the Rutherford butler of thirty odd years, stood in the doorway, his tall, spare frame and lined visage reminiscent of happier times in days long past. But the advance of age had left its mark. Once possessed of a head of hair with equal amounts of gray and brown, his hair now rivaled the unadulterated white of Father Christmas. And his stature, which formerly would have been the envy of any uniformed man, now gently rounded at the shoulders, proving once again just how time spared no one.

Given he was a man disposed to typical English butler demeanor, she'd never imagined he had it in his personal repertoire to blanch, but that is precisely what he did upon viewing her. He said nothing for several seconds, simply stared, his eyes wide and unblinking. Charlotte stifled a laugh—one of the nervous sort— fearing any attempt at speech would cause her to dissolve into a heap of polka dot skirts at his feet.

Behind her, a horse whinnied and stomped its hooves and birds continued their cheerful chirping while Reeves appeared to be struggling to find his tongue. At length, he exclaimed softly, "Lady Charlotte." He spoke as if he believed she was but a vision and any undue noise would send her off into obscurity.

Charlotte managed a tremulous smile, tears pricking the corners of her eyes. "Hullo, Reeves. I-I'm delighted to see you looking so well." The greeting seemed hardly adequate, but she was at a loss to find something fitting to say after so long an absence. So sudden a departure.

Her voice appeared to galvanize him into action. Throwing open the door, he ushered her through an entrance hall as large as the ground floor of her townhouse and into the vestibule. She'd quite forgotten just how large an estate her brother owned.

"I fear we were not apprised of your arrival. Such a shame as, just this morning his lordship and her ladyship went into London with the children. However, Lady

Catherine is in residence. She will be happy that you've returned." Reeves never smiled, and that hadn't changed, but he did appear pleased to make the announcement.

"I hadn't time to send word of my coming." She'd naturally assumed everyone would be home with her sister doing so poorly. She was more than a little surprised that James had gone off to London and left Katie alone in the care of the servants—and no doubt the attending physician. Actually, it was inconceivable that he would do so.

Pivoting sharply to face the elderly butler, Charlotte laid a restraining hand on his black clad arm as he made a move to relieve her of her pelisse. "Reeves, can you tell me anything of my sister's condition?"

Reeves' stilled at her touch. Lowering his hands to his sides, he stared down at her, his brows furrowed. After a pause, the deep creases in his forehead eased to mere lines. "If you're speaking of that rather nasty cold she fell ill with the month past, then I can assure you she has since fully recovered."

A cold?

The doctor has done all he can for her. If she recovers it will be by the grace of God.

She could hear Lucas's words as though he'd spoken them yesterday. Not even the severest of colds rose to that criticality.

Before she had an opportunity to question Reeves further, the scramble of feet and a high-pitched squeal drew her attention to the top of the double mahogany staircase.

Her sister stood in the middle of the first floor landing clutching the balustrade, her form poised for flight. "Charlotte, is that really you?" Katie cried. Then in a blur of pale green muslin, she took the right set of stairs with all the refinement of a horde of marauding boars. Her fingers skimmed and skipped over the polished mahogany banister as her skirt fluttered and quivered under the breeze of her stampeding steps.

Transfixed by the first sight of her twin in nearly five years as she flew down the stairs, Charlotte could neither move nor speak.

Katie wasn't ailing.

At least Charlotte had never seen a person whose survival was said to have hinged on God's mercy with so much bounce and pep, her cheeks flushed with the healthy hue of breathless excitement, not the ravages of fever. No, her sister looked as vital and healthy as any twenty-three year old woman could.

After a fortnight of anticipating the worst and ardent prayers that she'd arrive to find her sister at least on the verge of recovery, a tidal wave of emotion washed over her, and soon Charlotte was moving, her feet carrying her forward without conscious effort or thought.

"Oh Lottie, Lottie. You've come back," her sister cried before launching herself into her arms. "Lord, how I've missed you."

Charlotte choked out a sob at the use of her

childhood name as they embraced at the foot of the staircase, clinging to one another under a deluge of shared tears. Joy, relief, and the pain of their long separation had Charlotte trembling uncontrollably. The last time they'd held each other this tightly, they had been frightened five-year-old orphans just arrived at the boarding school. Save a father who'd ensured for only their financial welfare, they'd been very much alone in the world.

"Oh God, I thought you—" Charlotte broke off abruptly when her sister turned a tear-stained face to her, her joy a living breathing entity. How could she now admit she'd returned because she'd thought her near death's door? She could not.

"Thought I was what?" Katie asked in a voice choked with tears.

"I thought perhaps I wouldn't find you home," Charlotte quickly improvised. "Oh Katie, how I missed you too, so very much."

Katie's breaths came in pants and half sobs, her arms tightening around Charlotte's waist until she could scarce draw a breath. How long they stood holding each other, she didn't know. But for those finite moments, time seemed to stand still.

After she caught her breath, and her sister was no longer gasping as if she'd been running too hard and too long, Charlotte loosened her hold and drew back to take in a face so dearly familiar and identical to her own. With them, their differences lay beneath the surface.

Sky blue eyes fringed with thick lashes gazed back at her. Eyes glassy with tears. In all the jostling and excitement, ringlets of burnished gold curls had come dislodged from what had to be a small army of pins securing her sister's chignon. How well Charlotte knew what it took to keep the thick mane properly tamed and presentable.

Katie reached out to cradle Charlotte's cheek in her palm, her touch almost reverent. "Where—when–why didn't you say anything about coming home in your last letter?"

"The decision was very last minute," Charlotte whispered in a voice equally thick with emotion as her twin's.

After brushing the crest of Charlotte's cheek with her thumb, Katie dropped her hand to her side. "I hope you realize that James and Missy will be beside themselves when I send word of your return," she chided gently. "They're to stay in London a week. Of course, I'll have to send word express that you've returned. I expect they'll be home tomorrow or soon after."

"I know and I'm disappointed too, but in a way I'm happy it's just the two of us—at least for today."

Katie smiled, her face flushed pink with pleasure. After several seconds of contented silence, she took a step back and began a critical appraisal of Charlotte's figure, commencing at the ruffled collar of her blue and yellow wool-traveling suit. Her expression sobered the further her gaze continued downward. "You're too thin.

14

Why, I must outweigh you by a good half a stone."

"Perhaps a little. I've recently dropped some weight." The stress of thinking one's sister hovered on the brink of death tended to kill one's appetite. Of course, that was something she couldn't now admit to her twin.

"We'll have to fatten you up a bit. It's obvious you haven't been taking proper care of yourself," Katie stated crisply, eyeing the dress at her waist, which several weeks ago had cinched it nicely instead of bunching with excess fabric as it did now.

"You haven't changed a bit, still just as bossy as ever," Charlotte teased, attempting to lighten the mood. Her sister would have time to reproach about her inadequate diet later. Desperate to hold off the questions sure to come, she turned to her surroundings. Her gaze swept the three-storey vestibule and down the wide corridor of the picture gallery ahead. "Though the same can't be said of this place. I would hardly recognize it anymore."

Katie came immediately to her side and hooked her arm through hers as if she couldn't bear any physical distance between them. Following the direction of Charlotte's gaze, she said, "Yes, Missy redecorated three summers ago. I'm proud to say I did have a small hand in the effort. I selected the chandelier." Her sister angled them toward the front and pointed at the elaborate crystal and glass lighting fixture soaring high above the entryway. "A fine choice if I daresay."

Charlotte nodded her agreement. Her sister had always had exquisite taste.

"Missy insisted on a décor more suited to children. The rugs were purchased when the floors met with one too many of her treasured Wedgwood vases. Marble tends to be terribly unforgiving that way." She emitted an airy chuckle. "But the alterations have added a warmth that was lacking before. Don't you think it looks and feels more like a home and less like a museum than when the dowager lived here?"

Charlotte nodded mutely as a frisson of fear coursed the length of her spine at the mention of the dowager. She didn't want to think about her.

Slowly, she lowered her gaze to admire the Persian rug beneath her booted feet, and continued on to take in silk-papered walls done in dark green. Two walnut tables inlaid with a lighter wood, and several chairs with cushioned seats in which a weary bottom might actually find comfort also graced the hall.

"Yes, it certainly does."

Months after the death of their father, James's mother, the dowager Countess of Windmere, moved to Devon and James took possession of the manor. Charlotte had found the place as cold and sterile as its previous occupant. Although they had never been formally introduced, the dowager had made no secret of her loathing for Charlotte and Katie. But given they were the illegitimate issue of the woman's husband and born only months after her youngest son, her feelings were understandable and expected. However, the dowager had carried her hatred too far. The letter and the threat had revealed her truly vindictive side.

"While I was sad for James and Christopher when she passed away, I must admit to a sense of relief knowing our paths would never cross again."

Charlotte's next breath emerged a serrated gasp. Her head snapped to the side and she stared at Katie, mouth agape. "She is dead?" she asked in a hushed whisper.

Her sister sent her a puzzled frown, her winged brows collecting over a slender nose. "Surely you can't be distressed?" Katie asked, clearly mistaking her shock for sadness. "You know how I normally refrain from the use of clichés, but truly that woman has been the bane of my existence. If you had remained, you would have been similarly affected. I'm certain if not for that wretched woman, I would have married ages ago. But no, she refused to allow anyone to forget I was James's illegitimate sister. Not at all good enough for their precious sons."

Charlotte didn't respond immediately, still trying to digest the enormity of what she'd just learned. Dare she hope with the dowager gone, so too was the threat she had posed to everyone Charlotte loved?

"When—when did she die?" If she died recently, there was still time for the truth to come out if she'd confided in anyone.

"Early last year. I would have told you had I an address to send my correspondence to," Katie replied a

17

note of censure in her voice.

For almost an entire year. The length of time gave Charlotte great hope. James and Missy were in London with the children, and presumably still welcome members of Society. Certainly if the dowager had shared the information, something would have surfaced by now. It appeared she had taken it with her to her grave. She shot Katie a glance. Their secret was safe.

"I imagine it must have been a very difficult time for James and Christopher." This Charlotte could say with all honesty.

Her sister gave her a sidelong look. "I feared you were going to start spouting empty platitudes about how sorry you are that she's gone. She was a simply horrible woman, and I haven't missed her one little bit."

No, Charlotte couldn't have lied to her sister about that. She wasn't that good an actress. "As I said before, you haven't changed at all," she said dryly. Her sister didn't believe in being agreeable for propriety's sake.

Katie flashed an infectious grin. "And why should I change? As I recall it was the only way anyone could tell us apart. Should I become kind and agreeable, I could very well be mistaken for you."

"And we certainly wouldn't want that," Charlotte replied, feeling lighter than she had in years. Such a shame that the death of someone close to the brothers she loved had removed an enormous weight from her. "Although, that happened often enough when we first came to live with James."

18

For their newly discovered brother and his bride, telling her and Katie apart had come down to the simple matter of her sister's birthmark—a tiny mole on the nape of her neck. The memory of Missy craning her neck in a not so subtle attempt to determine the existence—or lack thereof—of said birthmark brought a small smile to Charlotte's face, eliciting a stark sense of nostalgia.

"Yes, the only person who never confused us was Al—" Katie broke off abruptly, as her eyes flashed wide with alarm. "I didn't mean to-I mean...."

Tears stung Charlotte's eyes and her chest constricted. Pulling her sister's arm tighter against her side, she whispered, "It's fine. I won't break at the mention of his name. Truly. Anyway, it was I who...." She swallowed the lump that had formed in her throat. "Alex has always been a big part of our—your life. I certainly don't expect you to change anything to suit me."

With a tiny nod, Katie drew Charlotte into the circle of her arms for a gentle hug before setting her away. "Come, you must be famished. Off with your cloak and I shall have the cook prepare you something to eat. Then you can tell me everything that has happened to you in these last five years. I assume you hired a hackney from the station in town."

Without giving Charlotte an opportunity to respond, her sister turned to Reeves, who stood far enough away as to allow them privacy, but close enough to be summoned to duty forthwith. "Reeves, please have the footmen retrieve my sister's belongings from the coach."

"No!" The response sprang sharp and unbidden from Charlotte's mouth. Even she could hear the panic threading her tone.

Both the butler and her twin treated her to a look of surprise.

"I mean not yet. Katie, there is something I need to tell you—"

A movement, a figure, in the corner of her vision halted her speech. Charlotte shifted her gaze. Her breath and her world came to a shuddering halt.

Alex.

He rounded the stretch of hall leading from the study. Their eyes met across a distance of some forty feet.

Her breath left her completely then. The air surrounding her became charged and hot.

His stride might have faltered but he recovered so swiftly, she couldn't be certain she hadn't imagined it.

Charlotte stood frozen, ensnared as deftly and completely as a rabbit in the presence of a rattler preparing to strike. She watched as he proceeded down the seemingly endless corridor toward her.

Senses starved for the flesh and blood man greedily tried to take him in all at once, hoarding away every minute detail to take back with her to feed the lonely nights when dreams and memories were all she'd have…and yet still not enough.

Save the measured fall of his footsteps, silence

reigned with a parasitic presence that made speech a novelty and breathing a luxury. Charlotte could do nothing but wait in statue-like stillness while her heart picked up its pace. To even blink would have been unimaginable.

As he drew closer, she began to make out the subtle changes time had wrought in his visage.

In appearance, he looked much the same as the man she'd known and loved—loved still. With hair the black and shine of obsidian brushing the collar of his tan morning coat, and the delicious little dimple in his chin, he had always been surfeit in looks. But the Alex of old had possessed a wicked sort of charm. His smile, lazy and hinting at deeper passions, had caused the palpitation of many a female hearts. Upon their betrothal announcement, the gossip sheets had stated the sound of those very same hearts breaking could be heard from Cornwall to Northumberland.

At present, however, it appeared no smile would dare venture near his lips. Faint lines bracketed his full mouth, the surrounding skin taut and unforgiving in its sternness. And there was an iciness in his expression that pierced her heart with a corresponding blast of cold. He even carried his lean muscular frame with an aloofness, tight and very controlled.

Any hope that she would find in him a smidgeon of warmth, an inkling of the affection he'd once felt for her, wilted and died under his regard. Yet she remained resolute as he advanced upon her, awaiting the first words they would exchange since the day before what should have been their wedding day.

With his every step, her anxiety climbed and her heart stumbled over the hurdle an ocean and five years had created. Twenty steps separating them became ten and then five. He stopped just shy of an arm's length of her. Continuing to imprison her with his silver-eyed gaze, he finally spoke. "I see you have company."

Charlotte nearly wept at the sound of his voice, a smoky baritone. Perhaps that was the reason it took her a moment to comprehend he was speaking to Katie and not her. That it was she to whom he referred to as 'company'.

"Alex, I had no idea you were here," her sister said with an uncharacteristic catch in her voice.

After a taut silence, he yanked his gaze from Charlotte's and turned to include her sister in his regard as well as his address. "I instructed Reeves not to disturb you when I arrived. I'm just here to retrieve some documents your brother left for me."

It was then Charlotte noticed the large envelope clutched in his hand.

"Um, Alex, Char-Charlotte has ju-just now arrived."

Never had Charlotte heard her sister stammer so. Given the circumstances, it was *she* who should be rattled and out of sorts. She was all that and more.

"So I see," he replied in clipped tones, keeping his gaze averted from her. As telling and deliberate a gesture as she'd ever witnessed.

Charlotte knew then she would have to initiate any form of communication between them. And who else should do it if not her.

"Hullo, Alex," she said, finding her courage and her voice. But never had two words taken so much effort to speak.

His jaw firmed, his nostrils flared and an ominous stillness settled over him. A moment later he gave her sister a brisk nod. "I shall leave you to your guest. Good day, Catherine." His gaze did not venture in her direction again. It was as if, to him, she'd ceased to exist.

Charlotte turned to watch as his long strides carried him across the wool rugs on the marble floors, through the entrance hall, and out the front door.

Lord, he wouldn't even acknowledge her. She'd have preferred he'd railed and cursed her. She'd rather he'd shaken her like a ragdoll. Anything would have been better than being so ignored.

The weight of her sister's hand settled on the curve of her shoulder, comforting and warm. "He is in shock. You must give him time to adjust to your...presence." Though the words were meant to placate her, Katie's tone held a hint of something else, a pained sort of despair. As if she herself was experiencing Charlotte's hurt.

But Charlotte now knew he would never forgive her. The entire situation would simply grow ever more intolerable. The sooner she returned to America, the better it would be for everyone. To see him was to be constantly reminded of all she'd lost and all she'd had to walk away from. It would simply be too much.

"Where is he staying? The guesthouse? Have I just sent him in search of other accommodations?" Charlotte imagined he'd be departing the place shortly.

"Oh no, it's nothing like that. Alex purchased the Grechen Manor two years back. Do you remember it?"

Charlotte briefly lowered her lids, only able to dip her head in response. Of course she remembered the Palladian style manor house with its portico, towering columns and lush green lawns. She'd fallen in love with it on sight. The house was no more than ten miles down the road, an easy distance by carriage or on horseback. Alex lived but a stone's throw away.

"Oh Lottie, you mustn't look so cast down." Catherine nudged her chin up with her fingertip. "So much has happened since you've been gone. Alex hasn't been the same since you left. You must be patient with him."

A blink sent a stream of tears down cheeks now cool to the touch. They landed on her sister's palm. "He despises me."

"Believe me my dear, he does not despise you. Isn't it obvious he's still hurt by the whole affair? That itself says a great deal about how much he loved you."

Loved her. The past not the present. He didn't love her anymore. And would he still have loved her if he knew the truth about her. Who she really was?

24

"Come now, you look positively fatigued. First we must get some food in you and then you can rest. I'll have to put off my interrogation until later."

Her sister's words had her stomach clenching in apprehension. There was one secret she had no choice but to reveal now, for it would become known soon enough.

"Katie, I didn't come back to England alone. There is someone I'm most desperate for you to meet."

~*~*~

She was back.

Alex descended the front steps toward his carriage, his pulse pounding a staccato beat. After two years of sobriety, he wanted—no needed—a drink. He needed enough to wipe her image clean from his mind. Which meant he'd have to consume the whole damn bottle. But thankfully not a drop of alcohol existed at his residence. Today he was safe, temptation of that sort well out of reach.

Though not impossible to acquire should his resolve crumble, a voice inside of him taunted. Alex ruthlessly quashed it. He'd come too far and worked too hard to be dragged down by that particular vice. By her.

Why the blazes had she come back? A damned eternity would have been soon enough to have to see her again.

Was she back for good? Was she married?

The questions crept insidiously into his thoughts, catching him unaware. Once years ago, he would have

25

sold his soul—and at times thought he had—for any news of her. How often had he lain in his bed and prayed she'd come back to him or wished he would wake up to discover his wedding day had just been a dream. A nightmare. Today the thought that only a few miles separated them made his blood run cold.

She was so damn beautiful. Though unwanted, the observation was in no way a compliment to her. It was simply a statement of fact. And if he dared flirt with facts, he would have to concede she was even more beautiful than before. At eighteen, she'd been a flower on the brink of bloom. Well, she had bloomed and was certain to be a danger to the gentlemen in Society. No doubt she was a danger to men everywhere. Lord how he wished those four years, ten months and three weeks hadn't been so kind to her.

Suddenly, the plaintive cry of a child rent the quiet of the April midday. Just about to bolt into his carriage, Alex's gloved hand stilled on the cool metal sides of the phaeton. Angling his head in the direction of the sound, he noted for the first time a hackney coach parked a fair distance behind his in the circular drive. No doubt her transport. And it appeared she hadn't come alone.

Without stopping to consider the injudiciousness of his actions, but compelled by a force beyond his control, Alex tossed the envelope onto the passenger seat of his phaeton and started toward the carriage, unsure of his purpose or what he hoped to learn.

He passed the idling driver without a glance, his

mind preoccupied.

Whose child was it? Not that any of this mattered to him. It did not. Despite his denials, he found himself peering into the dark green interior. Ensconced in the back was a woman, and tucked at her side sat a young boy, whom she spoke to in quiet, soothing tones.

"Is there something wrong with the child?" He was fully cognizant that he had no business asking the question and that the answer was none of his concern. None of that seemed to matter.

The woman's head snapped up at his voice revealing a breathtakingly beautiful face belonging to a young woman of no more than seventeen or eighteen years. With brown spiraling curls peeping from beneath her bonnet and a complexion that resembled his own tanned several hours in the sun, it was apparent she was of mixed blood. A mulatto.

"No sir, we is—are waiting for his mama," she replied in an accent that proclaimed her American origins.

She had a child.

Although Alex had prepared himself for such an answer, upon actually hearing it, he stiffened, his breath escaping between his lips in an audible rush.

Swallowing hard, he stared at the boy who sat crowded against the girl, a fisted hand rubbing his eyes as if he'd just awakened. Then the boy tipped his head back to gaze up at him. Alex staggered back a step, his stomach feeling as if it had plunged clear down to his toes.

When he was five, his mother had commissioned a portrait of him and his older brother, Charles. Vivid in his recollection were the three lashes he'd received that day from his father for some small infraction. It had never taken much for him to raise his father's ire—it still did not. The portrait borne of that unhappy incident in his young life hung in the gallery at Windsor Place, the Duke's seat and country estate. The child who peered up at him now, his blue eyes still drowsy with sleep, his hair a mop of blonde looping curls, could have been the six-year-old boy in the portrait.

The child peering up at him could have been his brother Charles.

CHAPTER TWO

"Who do you want me to meet?" Katie asked, her voice lowered to a whisper, ripe with curiosity. Then she gasped as if a scandalous thought had just occurred to her. Her blue eyes rounded as did her mouth. "Are you married? Have you a husband waiting out in the carriage?"

Charlotte drew in a deep breath, bracing herself. Her sister wouldn't be happy. Above all else, this would be yet further evidence of how much of her life she'd kept hidden from her. "No, not a husband, but a—"

Voices at the front entrance halted her revelation. Charlotte turned and watched in shocked disbelief as Alex, her maid Jillian, and Nicholas appeared in the doorway between the entryway and the vestibule, Reeves currently nowhere in sight.

"I've found a child in need of his mother," Alex announced, his gaze never wavering from hers as he approached.

Ever since Charlotte had made the decision to return to England, she'd anticipated and prepared for this moment. Well as much as a green soldier could prepare himself for the realities of war. Nothing, however, could have prepared her for the fear threatening to consume her whole. This was not the way Nicholas's introduction was supposed to occur. Like the only player on stage without a script or direction, she fell silent as her mind raced searching for the proper response. But search as she might, no words would come.

"Mama." Her son's exclamation was accompanied by the sound of tiny booted feet charging across the floor until he reached her side in a fever of breathlessness, his face stained with dried tears.

"Mama?" The same two-syllable word, yet her twin uttered it in an entirely different manner. "You have a son?"

Alex strode toward her with staggering nonchalance given he hadn't deigned to address her only minutes before. But his expression hadn't lost its cold inscrutability. His gaze darted to Nicholas, before settling on her once again.

Behind her, Katie sounded like an asthmatic trying to catch her breath but Charlotte could deal with only one calamity at a time. Alex had to come first.

Settling her hands protectively on her son's shoulders, she met Alex's stare as air inched its way into her lungs. You can do this. You must do this.

"When I heard him crying, I thought it best if I brought him inside," he said, halting in front of her. She could feel his condemnation emanating from his pores.

He spoke to her, yet still he did not greet her. Charlotte swallowed a lump of despair. I cannot do this.

Nicholas tipped his head back and stared up at Alex, who at six-foot-two inches tall loomed above him like a dark angel.

"You have a son?" This time her sister's voice held more than a trace of pique and hurt. Briefly, Charlotte regarded Jillian, who appeared oblivious to the enfolding drama, her hazel eyes soaking in the grandeur of her surroundings with awe.

Angling her head over her shoulder, Charlotte met her sister's gaze. "Katie, I'm sorry." Explanations—as much as she could offer—would have to wait.

Truly, this was not how she had envisioned—had planned the introduction of aunt to nephew.

"He's a handsome boy. I expect he resembles his father."

Turning back to him, Charlotte swallowed hard and felt the burn of a guilty blush suffuse her face, not exactly certain how she should respond to Alex's remark. It was plainly spoken and lacking in artifice, some of which she might have expected given their history. But most people thought Nicholas resembled her with his dark blonde locks and blue eyes. Most never bothered to look beyond those obvious similarities. Alex was unlike anyone she'd ever met, a fact she would be wise to remember.

"Yes, he does. Unfortunately, his father died before he was born." There, she'd done it, the first lie, the seedling of a multitude more. But then it wasn't as if this was chaste, uncharted grounds. One would assume she'd

31

be quite accomplished at it by now. Indeed, she was unquestionably a connoisseur should lying be raised to an art form—if indeed it was not.

While her sister's indrawn breath scalded Charlotte's ears, Alex continued to stare at her, his thickly fringed eyes devoid of emotion, his expression positively deadpan. "So you married?"

Only the faintest inflection in his tone indicated it was a question, and nothing in his voice hinted that asking had caused his heart to contract in anguish, as hers had done. He sounded politely inquiring, expressing no great necessity to actually know.

But to utter that particular lie aloud—to Alex—was more than her conscience or heart could bear. There did exist a limit to her duplicity. Charlotte inclined her head in a jerky nod, unable to hold his gaze. But if she thought he might challenge her, that somehow he'd seen through the veil of her deception, she couldn't tell by his expression.

Alex glanced down at Nicholas and only then did she see an infinitesimal warming in his silver-gray eyes. In a surprising move, he lowered to his haunches and extended his right hand to her son. Nicholas inched back against her skirts, shooting a quick look up at her as if to seek assurance as to the safe worthiness of the stranger. Too bewildered by Alex's unexpected show of kindness to do anything else, Charlotte responded with another jerky nod.

Nicholas slowly lifted his hand to find it quickly

enveloped in Alex's much larger one. "And your name, young man?"

Charlotte opened her mouth to answer, but it seemed her son had had the response primed and ready on the tip of his tongue.

"Nicholas."

"A pleasure to make your acquaintance, Nicholas," Alex said solemnly, giving her son's hand a firm yet gentle shake. Charlotte thought her heart would simply break in two.

"Thank you, sir."

"And how old are you?"

Charlotte's heartbeat thundered in her ears and her hand tightened on his slender shoulders. Before he could respond, she replied, "He will be four in July." Lie number two.

Releasing Nicholas's hand, Alex rose smoothly to his feet. "He's tall for three."

Her son was tall for four. He'd be tall like his father. A short silence followed his statement, as Charlotte couldn't bring herself to agree.

His gaze met hers. Guilt and a swell of wholly inappropriate emotions caused another wave of heat to flood her face in a mad rush.

Alex pulled out a gold fob and gave it a quick glance before returning it to his coat pocket. Inclining his head in a nod toward her son, he said, "It was a pleasure to meet you, Nicholas." He then directed his attention to Katie who had long gone silent behind her. "Good day, ladies."

The use of the term ladies should have signified her inclusion, but something in the fleeting look he gave her did not leave her with the feeling that he wished her well at all. In fact, behind his impenetrable stare, she was certain he wished her a trip to hell and back—or perhaps he'd rather she not return.

For the second time in the span of fifteen minutes, Alex took his leave of her and something inside her told her he'd do his utmost to avoid all contact with her in the future. She wanted to weep the same way she'd done when she had been the one to walk away all those years ago.

It was only after the distant click of the front door closing that Katie took those few steps to come to her side. "You were married and didn't say a word of it to me? Not in one of the twenty letters you've written over the years might you have mentioned a husband…and a son?" From her tone, it was difficult for Charlotte to discern whether her sister was more angry than hurt, but she estimated— or rather hoped—it was the former as that emotion was easier to handle.

Nicholas turned and looked up to view his aunt. He became wide-eyed and began frantically tugging on Charlotte's hand resting on his shoulder. "Mama, she looks like you," he exclaimed in a high voice.

With her eyes, Charlotte pleaded for her sister's understanding and cooperation. The last thing she wanted was to have this particular conversation in front of her son, her maid, and anyone else whose interest was piqued by a salacious bit of gossip.

Katie acknowledged her silent request with a brisk nod, before doing just as Alex had done, and going down on her haunches in front of her nephew.

"Do you remember when mama told you that I had a sister who looked exactly like me? Well, this is your Aunt Katie. Now be a good boy and say hello," Charlotte urged gently.

Tears gathered in her sister's eyes as she stared at Nicholas with a focused attention.

"Hullo, Aunt Katie," he whispered, staring at her with the same sort of fixation.

Her sister's fingers skimmed his face in feather light brushes. "Hullo, Nicholas," she said in a choked voice. "Would you mind terribly if I gave you a hug?"

Perhaps it was the familiarity of the face that eased Nicholas's usual reticence with strangers, for he gave a shy nod of assent without seeking the assurance he'd sought from her when Alex had offered him his hand. Quickly he was enfolded in her sister's arms, his own trapped at his side like a toy soldier. Nonetheless, he permitted her to hug him for a very long time.

~*~*~

The next hour passed in a blur of activity. Katie enthused over her nephew as if he were the greatest archeological find of all time. She hugged and petted him as much as Nicholas would permit, which was considerable given her son too seemed enthralled at the living and breathing creature whose face was the mirror image of his mother's.

Charlotte introduced Jillian to her sister. Relieved of her bonnet, the full glory of her maid's beauty caused Katie to halt and stare. A discernible blush appeared beneath Jillian's *café au lait* complexion. And Charlotte knew precisely what her sister was thinking; a servant that uncommonly pretty would be trouble in deuces and spades. But they would cope. They'd had to cope before.

Two footmen clad in liveries of the family colors, gold and green, were dispatched to collect their bags and trunks from the hackney. Nicholas would sleep in the nursery, and Jillian would sleep in the room next to the nursery until the children and their nanny returned. Charlotte was assigned her former bedchamber.

After they'd all eaten, Jillian volunteered to put a sleepy Nicholas down for his mid-afternoon nap. Charlotte dearly wished she could follow, but the look on her sister's face told her an explanation would not wait until after she'd rested.

Jillian and Nicholas had barely departed the dining room before Katie marched her down the hall and into the morning room. She steered her past the piano and harp, and dragged her down onto the chintz settee to take a seat beside her.

"You left because of what we discovered about our mother, didn't you?"

Charlotte took a deep fortifying breath, for she had to

An Heir of Deception

be convincing above all else. "That might have played
some part in my decision to leave, but it wasn't the
whole of it. I met a man two months prior to the
wedding. We fell in love."

Katie's jaw came unhinged, but soon shock gave
way to disbelief. In the narrowing of her eyes, suspicion
dawned clear and blue.

"I know it sounds extraordinary does it not? I mean
Alex had been the love of my life. But I realized what I
felt for him was a blind devotion. A case of mad
passion. Perhaps even the want of something I believed I
could never have. I mean truly, Alex interested in me? I
was not at all the kind of woman who could hold the
attentions of a man like him for long. Neil—that was his
name—was more…accessible. "

The disbelief faded from her sister's eyes and the
puzzlement returned.

Charlotte pressed on, relieved at the progress she'd
made. "In the end, although, I cared deeply for Alex, a
marriage between us would have been a mistake. But I
should not have waited so long to tell him and should
have had the courage to tell him to his face. For that I
will always be more ashamed and sorry than you can
ever imagine."

"But how could you leave me? Have you any idea
what we—what I went through these past years without
you, without being able to even write to you? One-sided
correspondence might suit your purposes but it didn't
mine."

37

Upon her return to England, Charlotte had planned to tell her sister about the letter threatening to expose the truth about who their mother was. But with the dowager gone, what good would it serve? Whose good would it serve? Katie had had a difficult enough time in society.

"If you knew how much I regret what I did but it had to be that way. I knew if I told you of my plans, you would tell James. And if James knew, it was only a matter of time before Alex discovered. That wasn't a risk I could take."

"But even if Alex did discover you'd fallen in love with someone else, it wouldn't have been the end of the world. You didn't have to run away."

Charlotte couldn't very well tell her it would indeed have been the end of the world as they all knew it. Alex would have seen right through her lies and gently coerced the truth from her. Following would have been a Rutherford family scandal far eclipsing the revelation of two illegitimate daughters. And Alex's titles would have been tarnished by his association with her. Everyone would have suffered. And then of course there was Nicholas...

"But why—"

"Katie darling," Charlotte implored, taking her sister's hand in hers, "no more questions on this subject for now. Please."

"Forgive me if I assumed as your sister, your twin, I would receive more consideration."

"Later, I will explain it all. Why I allowed so much

time to pass. Why I didn't tell you about Neil and Nicholas earlier. I promise I will." Charlotte gave her twin's hand a gentle squeeze. "But please don't press me on it now."

"From your maid's accent, I gather you've been residing in America?"

Charlotte gave a brief nod.

"James had investigators throughout the Continent but I don't believe he ever thought to look there." Katie spoke as if she were speaking to herself. "Have you come to stay?" she then asked, her cerulean blue eyes intent.

A heavy sigh escaped Charlotte's lips. That was a question she had yet to answer herself. She would like nothing better than to remain. The only person she would truly miss if she left America was Lucas, and he traveled to London on business often enough for them to remain in contact.

"I'm not certain."

Katie opened her mouth, and then quickly snapped it shut. Silence dragged for several long seconds before she spoke. "Whatever your reasons for your continued secrecy, I hope you know there is nothing you cannot tell me."

But there were also things that would only cause her sister needless distress, and Charlotte wouldn't inflict that pain upon her. It was enough that she knew and carried the shame of the secret.

"Katie, will you tell me about Alex?" Charlotte

asked in an abrupt change of topic. The question had festered inside her for too many years. She had to know.

Her sister's gaze sharpened just enough for Charlotte to don her mask and exclaim defensively, "What? I might not have married him, but I did care for him deeply. Naturally I care how he fared."

After a pause, Katie's mouth softened. "Well, to say your leaving hit him hard would be a vast understatement. He was like—well like I'd never seen him before. Frankly, he turned into a man I never care to see again."

A needlelike sting of pain accompanied every beat of Charlotte's heart upon hearing her sister's words. She'd wanted to know but now she wasn't certain. But her insatiable need to fill the gaps of those years without him urged her to delve in true masochistic fashion.

"What did he do?"

Katie swallowed, briefly looking down at their joined hands. "The truth isn't pretty and may be difficult for you to hear. Are you sure you want to know?" she asked, looking Charlotte in the eye.

Charlotte held a breath and nodded, steeling herself for what was to come.

After a prolonged sigh, Katie began. "He was already at the church when James told him. He left soon after, no doubt in shock and grief. James was left to inform everyone the wedding was off. Of course, he was also frantic with worry. We all were." Censure was blatant in her sister's tone. Charlotte squeezed her hands, attempting to convey just how sorry she was to have caused them even a moment of distress.

"After a day or so Alex joined James, Thomas, Mr. Wendell and Lord Bradford in the search for you."

Charlotte briefly closed her eyes. These were the things she'd tried so hard not to think about. Her family, her friends searching for her. Worrying themselves over her. Only the knowledge that she'd saved them from certain social ostracism and grief made the ordeal bearable. And of course, then Nicholas had come, needing her just as much as she'd needed him.

"Oh, they were all quite discreet about the matter. To this day everyone believes you're residing somewhere in the north of England. James wanted it so. The gossip surrounding your departure must have kept every printing press running non-stop for well over a year. He had no desire to feed the frenzy by admitting that we had no idea where you were. Anyway, when your first letter arrived two weeks later, Alex abandoned the search. I believe it was then he was convinced you had left of your own volition. It probably would have been easier for him if he thought you'd been taken by force."

Katie sighed and extricated her hand from hers. Charlotte instantly missed the warmth of her touch. "After hearing you were settling into your new home, he seemed to close himself off entirely. He wasn't sad anymore he was just…empty. Then he started drinking. And carousing."

Charlotte bolted to her feet, her moiré silk skirt

sweeping the low center table of knotted pine. She simply couldn't bear to hear anymore. The pain inside her was excruciating and blinding. "I see. You needn't tell me anymore," she said, trying not to choke on her words. She failed utterly.

Katie arose, treating her to a look of concern. "It is difficult to hear is it not? It was even more difficult to watch, and I didn't witness the half of it. You have no idea how many years James and Thomas spent beside themselves trying to save Alex from himself."

Charlotte closed her eyes, willing away the images of Alex lost in the stupor of drink as he caroused about town in quest of a warm willing female. And he'd no doubt found them to be had by the droves. But the images persisted with unforgiving relentlessness. She bit back a wave of nausea.

"Darling, you look pea green. Are you all right?"

Determinedly, Charlotte mentally shook it off, opening her eyes to take in the worried expression on her sister's face. "You did warn me it would be hard to hear." Agonizing, excruciating were more apt terms.

"Alex loved you. He took it exceptionally bad."

"And now? How is he now?" Silly as it was, what she really wanted to ask was did he ever talk about her? When had he stopped missing her? Within weeks, months, years?

Her sister gave a sad smile. "Well, he doesn't drink anymore. Not one drop. Gave it up entirely."

Thank God! Her guilt was suffocating enough. "Has

42

he married?" Charlotte hadn't meant to ask, in her heart was afraid to know. But there it was, her insatiable need to know everything about him exerting its control.

"Would it assuage your guilt and make you feel better to know he's married with a brood of children?" Katie asked, compassion in her eyes.

God no. It would destroy her. But she had no claims on him. She was the last person who should begrudge him happiness, even in the arms of another woman.

Turning from her sister, Charlotte advanced to the bay window. "Perhaps a little." This time she couldn't look her sister in the eye when she voiced the lie. Anyway, it was how her sister would expect her to feel given she'd just admitted she hadn't truly been in love with him.

"Then you'll be disappointed to hear he remains single. But all signs indicate it won't be for much longer as it appears he intends to ask Lady Mary, the Earl of Cranford's daughter, for her hand. The ton is expecting a betrothal announcement before the end of the Season."

Charlotte couldn't see the beauty in the profusion of budding daisies and violets landscaping the front lawn for the pain and grief swelling her heart. Ready to send her to her knees. But truly, it was a small miracle he wasn't already wed with several children by now.

"I see." Charlotte paused. "Well I wish him well." *And she did. She sincerely did.* It would be utterly selfish of her to begrudge him happiness with someone else. And by God she wasn't selfish. Her absence from his life attested to the fact. Marrying him would have been selfish.

"Charlotte, do you know what I believe?" Katie said softly from behind. She hadn't even heard her approach.

Charlotte turned. Her sister took her cold hand in hers and looked her in the eye. "I don't for a moment believe there was ever another man—this husband. And I don't believe you left because you didn't love Alex."

Stunned, Charlotte went stiff, her spine ramrod straight, feeling vulnerable and exposed. "What?"

Katie's mouth curved into a sad smile. "My dear, do give me some credit. I've known you all your life. Perhaps, the story you most convincingly spoon-fed me would have fooled strangers, acquaintances, and perhaps even James and Missy. But this is me. We occupied the same womb for nine months and bedchambers for fifteen years. You would have walked barefoot across the desert for Alex. And as for finding someone else? You had eyes for only him, which would have made that impossible. You loved him then and I'm quite convinced the years apart haven't changed that one little bit."

It should have been a diatribe, for Charlotte had lied to her, but it was not. Katie had exposed her web of well-rehearsed lies in calm, gentle tones, her only proof being her twin's intimate knowledge of her.

Charlotte briefly thought of issuing an emphatic denial but the lure of understanding in her sister's eyes had her head dropping as if her neck could no longer support its weight. Her admission conveyed the truth without a single spoken word.

CHAPTER THREE

Alex returned home and executed a swift change of clothes. His waistcoat suffered the loss of three of its four shanked, brass buttons. His rage ripped his linen shirt near the seam of the arm. He savaged the button closure of his trousers with his impatience. His drawers were the lone garment to survive the ordeal unscathed. He tamped down his anger long enough to ensure donning his riding clothes was a much less destructive affair.

He made good time getting to the stables, his long strides clashing with hard earth. Minutes later he sat bent over Shalais, his favorite Arabian mare, his gloved hands closed tight about the reins, flying across Reading's flat grassy terrain with the wind at his back.

With his every labored breath and every stretch of dirt kicked up by Shalais's hooves, he tried not to think about her. Since the moment he'd left, he had successfully pushed her image and memories of her as far back into the dark recess of his mind as they would go. But her image and the memories would not go willingly, refusing to be bowed by the strength of his will.

Little by little, they seeped back into the forefront of his thoughts as his gray-stoned manor house shrank against the backdrop of a deceptively cloudless, sunlit sky. She had returned bringing with her ugly and unforgivable lies, effectively darkening the skies like a swarm of locusts.

Dusty rose lips, just as soft and full as he remembered from countless dreams, looked too tempting to be the vehicle of such egregious lies. But those same lips had lied to him before. *I love you. Yes Alex, I'll marry you. I can't imagine my life without you.*

With a squeeze of his thighs, Alex urged Shalais into a full out gallop, trying to expend himself physically to quell the lure of oblivion a glass of alcohol could bring. He needed exhaustion enough to prevent him from the insanity of barreling a path through heavily wooded trees and underbrush to return to Rutherford Manor and force the truth from those same lying lips.

For years his feelings for her had drifted on the plane of indifference. He ceased to care where she was, what she did, and he never allowed himself to even venture near thoughts of with whom. Her return upended his long dormant emotions. His hatred now pulsed with new life, a new reason for its existence. Alex had never thought he could—would—ever despise anyone more than he did his father. Today he discovered he was wrong.

He returned to the house two hours later sweaty and hot. He was greeted by his rather anxious looking butler,

Alfred, who approached him the moment Alex stepped a dusty booted foot in the corridor leading to the main part of the house.

Alfred's powdered wig and severe black garb should have demanded a mien of stoicism, instead of the wringing-of-the-hands look on his face.

"My lord, Lord Cranford is awaiting you in the withdrawing room." Alfred had a tendency to speak as if he'd lived a century ago.

Alex quirked a brow. "Pardon?" he asked sharply, taking a moment to digest his shock. *What the hell is he doing here?* He almost blurted out the question, but good manners—at least the vestiges of those he still ascribed to—prevented him from doing so.

"My lord, he was quite insistent on awaiting your return."

The Earl of Cranford, Lady Mary's father, was definitely one of the last persons Alex wished to see today of all days.

"Please tell him I'll be with him shortly. As you can see, I'm not fit for company," Alex replied with a dismissive nod.

"Yes, sir," Alfred said with a bow before he strode off.

Twenty minutes later, Alex presented himself in the drawing room, freshly bathed and dressed from head to toe in cotton and wool in a brown as sober as his mood.

"Ah, Cartwright," Lord Cranford said upon his entrance, slowly rising to his feet with the help of a mahogany cane, his bare hand proffered in greeting. "I hope I haven't inconvenienced you by calling without an invitation." His jowls quivered from the force of his smile, which stretched across a small narrow face unbalanced by the leftward hook of his nose.

Alex forced a smile, taking the earl's hand in a brief handshake. "I hope you weren't terribly inconvenienced by the wait," he said, smoothly evading the question.

"Think nothing of it. I passed the time comfortably. I hope you won't mind if I sit. My knees have been paining me all day. A sure sign of rain tomorrow." The earl renewed his place on the brushed velvet sofa and although Alex would have preferred to stand, he followed suit and took up a seat in a wing-backed chair. There wouldn't be anything particularly pleasant about the coming conversation.

"Can I offer you something to drink or perhaps something to eat?" Alex asked.

Lord Cranford dismissed his offer with a negligent toss of his hand, the diamond on his signet ring glinting as it caught the sunlight pouring through the window behind him. "Your man saw to my needs. I couldn't eat another bite."

Which meant his wait had been considerable, possibly over an hour. Better to get the damn thing over with. "So to what do I owe to this call, my lord?"

The earl cleared his throat, straightened his legs with a slight wince and shot a look about the spacious drawing room before returning his gaze to Alex.

"Cartwright, how long has it been since you began calling on my daughter? Three, perhaps four months?"

"No more than three months if I remember correctly," Alex replied blithely. He hadn't been wrong in his thoughts. The earl had come to press his own suit.

"Yes, yes indeed. Just as I thought. One might consider three months ample time to decide on the suitability of a person might one not?" he said, inclining his head toward Alex as if to compel him to agree.

"Indeed, I believe three months might be more than ample time to make a judgment on such matter." It certainly had been for him. Alex thought of the emerald betrothal ring in his master suite upstairs. He'd purchased it with every intention of asking Lady Mary for her hand three weeks ago. But a day's delay had slipped quickly and all too easily, until soon he could count the delay by weeks instead of days. Now, given the change in circumstances, he was more than a little relieved he hadn't gone through with it. A betrothal would have been a nightmare of a predicament to extricate himself from.

Lord Cranford made a pleased sound, like the purr of a tiger, deep in his throat. He smiled again, showing off a row of white, slightly crooked teeth. "Ah, very good. I'm happy to hear. Then I assume I can expect a call from you before too long. I'm sure you know my Mary comes with quite a substantial dowry. Not to say, my good man," he hastened to add in a jovial tone, "that you are in need of it. Why, to your fortune, you no doubt see it as but a paltry sum."

Alex's mouth twitched, not quite a smile or a frown. When had thirty thousand pounds ever been considered paltry? The earl was being coy. "My lord, am I being pressed to fish or cut bait?" he asked blandly.

A wash of red suffused a complexion that probably hadn't been touched by sunlight in years. The earl appeared taken aback and didn't speak for several moments, eyeing Alex as if attempting to gauge the true inference of the question.

"What I'm attempting to convey, my lord, is that my daughter is much sought after." He said it with all the pomposity of a father who knew his daughter's worth.

Indeed, thirty thousand pounds.

"Many men have already approached me for her hand. She is of course, partial to your attentions, but she won't wait around forever. I'm merely urging you to press your advantage."

In other words, you have the advantage because you are excessively wealthy and heir to one of the oldest and most powerful dukedoms in all of England.

Alex had long since become familiar with aristocratic speak: the polite way to express one's single-minded ambition for money and position.

He tempered a wry smile at the earl's equating three months to forever as he was certain it would not be well received. "Then I would urge your daughter not to refuse any further marriage offers on my account."

Lord Cranford's eyes widened and his jowls shook

this time from the force of his inhalation. Bending his knees, he clambered unsteadily to his feet without the assistance of his cane or a wince even when his lower leg banged against the curved leg of the rosewood table. What followed was a silence that strained every bit of civility in his narrow-eyed countenance.

"Are you telling me you have no intention of asking my daughter for her hand?"

Alex pushed to his feet and with his half foot height advantage had an eagle's view of the bits of pink scalp peeking through the earl's gray thinning hair.

"I don't believe we would make a good match." Another face appeared in his mind's eye. One with dark gold ringlets and eyes the blue of the Mediterranean Sea. How apropos she'd returned and resumed where she'd left off—wreaking havoc on almost everything in his life. But good God, this time he'd make sure she paid.

Alex could tell by the venomous look in Lord Cranford's brown eyes that the man would like nothing better than to be his physical superior. His hands, much like the rest of his slight frame, shook with rage. "Not make a good match? You insolent little cur, you won't find another better than my Mary."

"Then I shall consider that my loss." Lady Mary was lovely and would have made an adequate wife, carrying out the duties of a duchess with aristocratic aplomb. But she certainly wasn't irreplaceable. No woman was. Many others would fill the role just as nicely. What annoyed him was the inconvenience of having to begin the ordeal of a courtship again after he'd concluded the whole affair with *her*.

"You are a—"

"And while I understand your anger, beg I remind you, my lord, I made no promises to either you or your daughter."

"You are nothing but a—"

"I will bid you adieu before you say something you will no doubt come to regret." Alex turned to one of the footman who never ventured far when he entertained guests—although that itself was a rarity—and now stood framed in the opening of the drawing room. "Please see the earl out."

While Lord Cranford sputtered in growing affront, Alex quietly departed.

Five years ago, he would have felt more than a pinch of remorse, for despite his avowal to the contrary, his manner would have led any parent to believe marriage would be the result of his attentions to their daughter. Today he couldn't summon up any emotion beyond irritation. And Lady Mary would hardly suffer. As her father had been eager to point out, she had a litter of men vying for her hand.

Alex made his way to his study, a place where he could bar the outside world from entry. But he didn't bar the door, he merely closed it, instinctively crossing the room to the sideboard. He pulled himself up with a vigorous shake of his head just as his hand reached for the crystal decanter, the fingers of his other hand already curved in anticipation of the glass.

The decanter was empty. The glass was naught but a decorative piece of etched crystal. Both had gone unused for two years. Alex abruptly dropped his arms, curled his hands into fists and strode over to the black leather armchair.

Memories of why he sought comfort in this particular room assailed him. It was in this very room he'd so often found solace—oblivion—at the bottom of a glass of rum. When all the rum was gone, he'd start on the whiskey. He had spent hours in a day—days on end sinking deeper and deeper under its spell. But not anymore. But damn, he needed a drink.

Damn her!

Tugging off his necktie, Alex pushed himself back into the sloping pocket of the high backed chair. His mouth curved into a cynical smile. The duke would think he's been handed heaven on earth when he learned about Nicholas. A living replica of his late beloved son would be like a dream come true. His mother, in her own dramatic fashion, would clutch her hands to her chest and cry copious tears. The ton, of course, would not only relish the scandal, they'd all but wallow in it. Something else to befall the future Duke of Hastings whose misfortunes had begun even before he'd been jilted at the altar. They'd practically rub their hands in glee.

Damn her!

This time, Alex refused to allow it to get that far.

"Alfred!"

Seconds later, his butler appeared in the doorway. "Yes sir?"

"Where is Conrad?" Alex inquired of his steward.

"He's—"

"Never mind that. Instruct him to arrange a meeting for me with Mr. Reynolds on the morrow. Tell him the matter is urgent." Bloody hell, at the moment not only did he require the counsel of a solicitor, he needed a vicar. Not to mention a constable to prevent him from wringing her deceitful, lying neck the next time they met, which would be soon enough. Sooner than she could ever imagine.

"I shall inform him directly, sir," Alfred replied, but made no move to leave.

Alex shot him an arched look. The last time his butler had worn that particular look of consternation was two and a half years ago, during one of Alex's more memorable drinking binges.

For failing to monitor the inventory of the rapidly diminishing alcohol closely enough, Alfred had suffered the indignity of having his capabilities, and worse yet, his hearing called into question. *Didn't you hear me when I told you I needed more rum? If you weren't so quick to run off, you'd take heed to half of the things I ask of you.* Sober, Alex had apologized for his tirade. That had been three days later.

Now, Alfred never missed a word or a syllable, always fastidiously awaiting a nod of dismissal before departing. Alex curtly obliged him.

Charlotte's chemise was not removed but caressed from her trembling body. Cotton linens woven so tightly, she thought it was satin or silk against her skin as she lay spread like a wanton on her back, her hands kneading and caressing sinewy muscles and damp flesh.

His fingers traced her nipple in slow, delicious concentration. Her back arched as her fingers bit deeper into his shoulders. Heat ripped a fiery path from her breasts, down the dip in her belly, and then set fire to the notch between her thighs. The wanting was excruciating madness, yet she knew she would die if he stopped.

"Does it feel good? Do you like it?" he asked, his voice rough with desire, his gray eyes dark with passion.

His breath fluttered on her nape and his finger continued its erotic dance with her nipple, reducing her to inarticulate gasps and moans.

She yearned. She writhed. So desperate was she to find surcease from the ache building and spiraling inside her, she was ready to beg for completion.

"Open for me," he said, before lowering his head, and drawing a pink, beaded nipple into his mouth. His cheeks hollowed as he began to suckle. The chamber echoed her cry of delight and her moan of satisfaction. With knees bent and her feet flat on the mattress, her legs fell open in eager anticipation and welcome.

Easing his finger into her opening, he found her slick, hot and tight. Soon another finger joined. Charlotte thrust her fisted hand into her mouth to muffle a scream. His withdrawal caused pleasure to scorch every inch of her sensitive inner flesh. Then he plunged back in. Helplessly, her hips began to move in counter point to his sumptuous thrusts. Soon his fingers weren't enough for either of them.

While he suckled her breast, pausing often to nip at her tip with teeth and tongue, he replaced his fingers with his erection. There was no easing or inexorable push, just a hard thrust, seating himself as far as he could go. Overwhelmed by the force of his possession, Charlotte whimpered, and then let out a gusty sigh of relief, of unadulterated pleasure. Her inner muscles clamped down on him hard.

He groaned low and long. "God, don't move." He wore an expression that ran the line between exquisite pleasure and torture. But Charlotte couldn't halt the undulation of her hips as she urged him deeper, hotter. Her soft pants filled the sex-humid air. His ragged groans joined hers as he set a rhythmic pace, thrusting heavily into her with long, smooth strokes. His tongue occupied her mouth like a lusty invader, kissing her until he learned all the hidden crevices of her hungry mouth and she did his.

For endless minutes, they mated with the intensity and avariciousness of new lovers, or old lovers who'd been too long apart. The chamber walls echoed their whimpers, moans and the hard slapping of damp flesh, intent on the climb to satisfaction.

As the precipice grew closer, he tore his mouth from hers, panting and making guttural sounds deep in his throat. His hands made forays around her breast and belly, roamed down further and found the hidden nub between her moist folds, and flicked it as he continued to pound into her, obliterating her every thought but the need for more. More of him. More of his touch. More of everything.

He shifted his hips, and the new angle and his finger on the source of her desire catapulted her up until she was soaring and exploding in a shuddering mass. She convulsed and heaved while he found his own release, before her glide back down to earth.

"Oh God, Alex. Alex," she chanted into his neck when he slumped atop her, his chest heaving for his next breath. Her hands clutched his muscled shoulders, and slid down to the sweaty expanse of his back to pull him close.

And then he was gone.

Her arms lay empty on the tangled white bedsheets. Charlotte reached out again with an urgency that bordered on desperation, endeavoring to stop the panic from consuming her. Again she found nothing. That's when the pain came and she embraced it with harsh, desolate sobs.

"Alex. Alex. Alex," she cried out in the dark.

Charlotte came awake with a start, her heart a stampede of horses thundering over America's wide-open plains. It took her a moment to get her bearings and catch her breath. She was in England in her old bedchamber. Tears wound their way down across her temples and settled in the cavity of her ears.

She had dreamed him again. Alex and their last time together. The tears rolled their course faster. The dream now came with a frequency that frightened her. For two weeks now, it had made its nightly sojourn into her sleep.

She'd woken up hot, her senses acute and overwrought, but now the coldness seeped into every pore despite the warmth of her bedchamber. The dreams always left her this way, chilled and dissatisfied. But tonight there was something else, a prickly uneasiness. It was then she realized the source of her disquiet wasn't the residual effects of her dream but something based firmly in reality.

Charlotte heard a slight movement to her right. She bolted upright, her hands clutching the counterpane close to her chest. In the darkened chamber, she could only make out the shape of someone—a man—reposed in the chair close to the fireplace.

Fear so effectively gripped her by the throat, all she could manage was a gurgled exhalation, not the bloodcurdling scream that would bring in the cavalry.

"Don't scream," a male voice instructed her softly.

For a moment Charlotte was convinced her ears were

playing some sort of cruel trick on her. Had she conjured his voice up from her dream? Was she that bad off?

He rose from the chair with an unmistakable ease and grace. Alex.

Seconds later, he was standing by the side of her bed, half his face illumed by the faint light from the fire burning on the grate. Not like the Alex of her dreams, this Alex was solid and real, and darkly forbidding.

"Alex—Alex what are you doing here?" Charlotte barely managed to croak out the question, hot all over once again.

She could feel his silver gaze scoring her, unreadable, unwavering. After a nerve-wracking pause, he asked in a voice both chilling and calm, "When did you intend to inform me you bore me a son?"

End of Sneak Peek